12 Days of Chri

And

The Heart of Christmas

12 Days of Christmas copyright © D. van de Merwe 2014
The Heart of Christmas copyright © D. van de Merwe 2017
All rights reserved

ISBN-13: 9781790901715

Extract taken from 'Twas the Night before Christmas' by Clement Clarke Moore

D. van de Merwe has asserted her right to be identified as the author of this work

This collection of short stories is a work of fiction. Names and characters are the product of the author's imagination and any resemblance to actual persons, living or dead, is entirely coincidental

Cover Design by
Angie Zambrano

Dedications

For the one I choose to spend my 12 days of Christmas with

For those who have been loved and lost this year
You shall be remembered

Content

12 Days of Christmas

The Eve of....

The dusty metal staircase proved unforgiving as Emma, armed with an unruly and cumbersome Christmas tree, struggled up three flights of stairs. Typically the lift was out of order, and being Christmas Eve was unlikely to be fixed in a hurry.

Emma, sweating and bruised and feeling entirely uncharitable given the time of year, huffed and puffed her way to the top, losing a million of the trees pine needles in the process.

She wished she'd remembered to get the tree the week before, like she'd promised her flatmate Jordie, when the lift had been working and the tree hadn't been such a mission to find. She'd ended up paying £50 for a tatty looking left-over four footer, when she'd had grandeurs of a smart and lush seven footer. Her excuse of working overtime at the surgery, up until Christmas Eve afternoon, had fallen on unsympathetic ears.

"I can't believe you've left it so late," Jordie had exclaimed at breakfast that morning. "What about all the post-its I left around the flat to remind you? All you had to do was get the Christmas tree. I've organised everything else, including the party tonight."

Not normally a disorganised person, Emma had felt a reasonable amount of guilt and found herself avoiding Jordie's eye.

"I'll get one today. I promise. You know I've been working hectic hours.

People don't stop being sick just because it's Christmas, you know."

Her justification was rewarded with a roll of the eyes from Jordie, who as a waitress in a coffee shop and an occasional children's entertainer, was far removed from the stresses of working in the NHS.

Emma split her shifts between working in the busy clinic's pharmacy and being a nurses' assistant. This really meant that she got all the boring and sometimes disgusting jobs: taking blood pressure, keeping the nurses' cupboards stocked and cleaning out toilets after patient's various 'accidents'. Add to that the stressful hours and immense amounts of paper work, Emma sometimes wondered how she'd kept her sanity. And yet she actually loved what she did and couldn't imagine doing anything else. She just wished, at times, that she worked hours that were more conducive to a normal lifestyle. It had been a long time since she'd had the energy to enjoy a night out with the girls, let alone a date with a guy.

With a deep breath Emma attempted the last few steps, heaving the prickly nightmare plant behind her. Her hands raw with scratches, she wondered why she hadn't worn gloves and then she wondered why she hadn't just bought a fake tree from the shop instead. But then she knew the answer to that. Real ones smelled of Christmas. They conjured up memories that fake ones didn't. Fake ones simply weren't the same. It was worth it for a few small injuries.

She looked back at the tree behind her. It looked a little worse for wear after the journey upstairs; branches stuck out at funny angles, one almost completely stripped of needles and the top of the tree was bent forty five degrees. Oh well, she thought, at least I bought one and at least I've finally reached the house.

She turned back to face the door of the flat, hand in one pocket to reach for the key, when she heard a door shut to her left and a gruff voice say,

"What the hell are you doing?"

She spun quickly, feeling guilty but not quite sure why, and faced the direction of the voice. A tall man stood just metres away, having exited the flat next door and watched her with a face of thunder. He waved his arm toward the staircase, covered in needles and muddy footprints (from her boots, which had trudged around a waterlogged pub garden where Del Boy's protege sold her what seemed like last year's reject trees).

"I hope you're going to clean all that up," he said, rather menacingly Emma thought.

"Of course, I am," she felt her heckles rise. Who did he think he was?

"I'm just going to take my tree indoors and then I'll come and sort it out, okay with you?" she retorted, hand on hip.

"Just make sure you do," he answered and frowned at the tree lying across the hall. "Did you seriously cart that all the way up here yourself?"

he added.

"No, my donkey did it for me. I'm the virgin Mary if you hadn't noticed," she replied, the sarcasm unlike her, but for him she'd make an exception.

"You don't look pregnant to me," he answered, a slight smile playing around his lips, which she found incredibly annoying.

"Well, thanks for that," she muttered and pulled the key out of her pocket rather ferociously.

"I'll help you if you want?"

"No thanks. Like you said, I'm not pregnant, so I think I can manage," Emma replied tartly and flounced through her open door before remembering the tree and cheeks reddening, she flounced back out and grabbed it by the trunk.

She tried to ignore the smile spreading across his features and slammed the door behind her. How rude was he! she thought as she stormed past the kitchen on the right and into the living room. Jordie was sitting watching Christmas TV shows and waved a hello without looking.

"I got the tree," Emma said, suddenly feeling deflated, tired and fed up with the whole festive season.

"Oh cool," Jordie replied, turning her head slightly for a look then quickly back a second time. "What on earth is that?"

"Don't you start. I've just had a talking to by the tree police next door," Emma sighed, stepping over the tree and heading to the kitchen for a much needed glass of wine.

"Who? Oh, you mean Jed, the new neighbour?" Jordie asked, realising Emma probably wouldn't be referring to sweet old Mrs Olban, their neighbour the other side, who'd more likely feed you Christmas cookies than tell you off over anything.

"What a stupid name," muttered Emma darkly, pouring herself a glass of white wine from the copious amounts lining the fridge shelves, awaiting the party that evening. She took a large sip then grabbed the washing up cloth and dustpan from beneath the sink and headed back out into the hall.

Fortunately Jed had gone and Emma took a deep relaxing breath as she began to clean up. She'd dealt with far worse at work; sick patients with a bark as bad as their bite, and yet this man had wound her up no end. It was because she was tired and stressed, she reasoned. She simply needed the holiday to rest and recover. Then, no amount of snotty comments from her neighbour would rock her.

Half an hour later, having retraced her steps and cleaned what felt like half the block of flats, Emma headed back through her door. The last thing she felt like now was a party. She groaned as she realised that was the least of her worries. The tree still needed to be put in a bucket and decorated. She'd need a bigger glass of wine.

*   *   *

Finally, just an hour before the party was due to start, Emma twirled the last bit of tinsel around the tree. She stepped back to admire her creation, but time constraints and being unable to find all the decorations had left it looking a little sparse at best. Never mind, she thought, that was all she could do in the circumstances.

She jumped into the shower, washing at breakneck speed, before literally running into the bedroom and dramatically throwing open her wardrobe. Several dresses were instantly discarded as being too showy. Emma wanted to be comfortable yet still look classy. She wasn't out to impress anyone, nor did she have the energy to doll herself up. A classic little black dress, hair quickly pinned up and a smudge of tinted moisturiser and mascara would have to do.

She pushed back thoughts of collapsing into bed with a good book and a frothy mug of chai and committed herself to the evening. Jordie had planned it all and Emma had promised to attend, so she'd just have to get on with it. She held her reddish blonde hair back in a messy bun and started to 'pin' away.

Within fifteen minutes Emma was ready and with a few minutes to spare, she helped herself to a top up of wine.

"Pace yourself," Jordie laughed, sitting at the breakfast bar wearing bold make up and a bright green dress, which suited her dark features.

"With the amount your friends drink, I'll be the least of your worries," Emma replied.

It was true, Jordie's friends could be a wild bunch and Emma had never really found much in common with them, yet Jordie herself had become a close friend over the nine months they'd been in a flat share together.

"So, who exactly are we expecting?" she asked, feeling it was better to be prepared.

"Oh, the usual," Jordie replied, digging a tortilla chip into a disgusting looking dip. "Anthony and Denise, Lucy, Jake and his brother what's-his-face, Kris, Jed, Sarah and Lloyd..." she reeled off, before Emma stopped her.

"Not Jed from next door?" Emma asked, heat rising up her neck from the sheer embarrassment and horror of their earlier unfortunate meeting.

"Yeah, he stopped by yesterday to introduce himself. He's just moved in, a few weeks back, but was travelling for work or something like that, so apologised for not introducing himself sooner. A really nice guy. I thought I'd invite him."

Typical, thought Emma, of course he'd be nice to Jordie and not to her. Jordie was gorgeous, tall and willowy with raven black hair and a complexion to die for. Short, frizzy haired Emma had just got an earful instead. That good book and mug of chai looked even more tempting and Emma had to literally force herself not to run in the direction of her room.

Before she'd had a chance to deal with her emotions a knock rattled the chain on the front door. Knowing it was Jed, seeing as the other guests would have to ring the buzzer to be let through the security door downstairs, Emma steeled herself for a terrible evening.

Jordie squealed with delight and practically flung herself toward the door as Emma instinctively stepped back.

"Hello Jed, I'm so glad you decided to come," Jordie schmoozed.

Jed stepped through the door and into the entrance hall. Emma noticed he was wearing the same red scarf and navy blue, thick coat as earlier and couldn't help but wonder if he'd bothered to change at all. Shaking herself from this uncharacteristic catty thought, she tried to put on a brave face and a welcoming smile.

"I see you managed to clean up the mess then," he stated, turning his attention to her.

Sod it, she thought.

"Yes, I'm perfectly capable of cleaning up after myself, thank you," she spat, arms folded. "Not that I need to be told off like I'm a six year old who's spilt paint all over the floor."

"Emma!" Jordie hissed, clearly mortified.

Jed looked confused for a split second, before changing the subject and handing Jordie a bottle of wine. Typical, Emma thought, he acts like butter wouldn't melt and I'm here looking ill mannered and disagreeable.

Fortunately more guests arrived before Emma could put her foot in it further and she quickly retreated to the corner of the room as the wilder friends and even wilder partying commenced. Nursing her fourth, and final (she knew her limits) glass of wine, she became increasingly uncomfortable with the loud shouting and carousing that the evening had descended into.

Dancing to bad Christmas songs and knocking back the free food and booze had given way to falling over, inappropriate jokes and drunken shouting. The Christmas tree had twice had to be rescued from toppling over and already a few had succumbed to the head in the toilet bowl routine. Emma had become quite adept at avoiding the dreaded mistletoe hanging in the hallway, despite several leering and clearly drunk attempts to kiss her from a few of the worse for wear.

While not a prude, tiredness and the longing for her bed had Emma wishing to be anywhere else but in the midst of her own living room. She'd long given up trying to make sensible conversation and the vast amount of people squashed into her flat had left her hot and desperate for fresh air. Unfortunately, she'd had to lock their balcony door through fear of losing a drunken guest over the rails, so fresh air was a limited commodity.

She pushed her way through the crowd and made her way to the kitchen. The room was empty, the remaining alcohol having been moved into the living room sometime before. She opened the small kitchen window wide and breathed in deeply. The winter chill hit her face full on and yet it was a pleasant relief to the oppressive air inside.

She closed her eyes to the icy wind pounding through the small gap and took a few precious minutes to cool down and unwind. As she finally and reluctantly turned away a figure walked into the kitchen. Her heart sank.

"Hi," said Jed, hovering uncertainly. He had an empty glass in his hand.

"The alcohol is back out there," she said, waving her arm in the general direction of the living room.

"No, I just came to get some water," he started toward the sink, in front of which she stood, and asked, "can I?"

She moved out of his way quickly, not liking how close he was to her, but not entirely sure why it should bother her so much. He was rude and annoying, for sure, but he could stand where he wanted surely?

He seemed to sense her tension and moved away, back towards the fridge and the other side of the room. He drank slowly, but didn't make any attempt to head back into the party. Emma was pleasantly surprised to see that he wasn't drunk like the others.

"I'm sorry about earlier, by the way," he said finally, having finished his drink and placing it on the kitchen counter.

"Oh?"

"The tree incident?" he answered slowly, looking confused again.

Great, she thought. He thinks I'm an idiot who can't remember what happened a few hours ago.

"Well you were very rude," she decided to give it all she had. "Not a great first impression to make when you're so new around here."

He looked surprised and shook his head slightly.

"Okay, I admit I was out of order," he said, holding his hands up in defeat. "I've just spent the last week laid up in bed with the flu and now I've finally started to feel something other than death warmed up and I get presented with a woman leaving half a forest in front of my doorstep."

"It wasn't anywhere near your doorstep," Emma said defensively, "though I'm sorry about the flu. It's been bad this year," she conceded.

"Thanks," he said, looking unsure, as if her sudden niceness was some sort of trick. Emma immediately felt guilty and decided it was time to make the peace.

"I'm Emma," she said.

"Jed, as you've probably already gathered," Jed replied, running a hand through his short brown hair.

"Jordie said she met you the other day, that you've just moved in but been out of town?" she didn't know why she was saying all this, but at least she was making conversation and they weren't arguing.

"Oh, sort of. I actually finished work a few weeks ago, but I had some meetings to attend... and then I was ill," he explained.

"Wow, what I'd do for several weeks off work at a time," Emma whistled through her teeth, trying to downplay the rising jealousy.

"I'm a lecturer, it comes with the territory," he shrugged.

"I'm in the medical field and we're lucky if we get a lunch break," she stated defensively, before remembering that she was meant to be biting her tongue.

"No wonder you know all about the flu then. You guys have it rough," he said, making eye contact properly for the first time.

Emma felt faint by a sudden and inexplicable twist in her gut. She had to look away.

"Yeah," was all she could manage.

They stood silently for a minute.

"Um..." Jed began, before being interrupted by an almighty crash in the living room.

Emma, dreading what she would find, bolted into the living room, Jed close behind. Jordie was sitting on the sofa laughing and hiccuping at Sarah, who'd finally managed to knocked over the Christmas tree, taking half the table of food with it.

Seeing her chance to wrap up the increasingly wayward evening, Emma took charge and began to usher out the party goers, calling taxis for whoever needed (which was pretty much all of them) and wishing them a Happy Christmas as they left.

Slamming the door behind the last drunken reveller, Emma turned her attention to Jordie, only to see Jed still hovering in the corner. He'd picked up the Christmas tree, tidied the food off the floor and had even taken the plates and various debris into the kitchen. Emma's heart warmed despite herself.

"Thanks Jed," she whispered, the tiredness, wine and emotions threatening to push her over the edge.

He looked from Emma to Jordie and back again.

"You girls need some sleep. It's Christmas tomorrow and you don't want to feel dreadful," he stated.

"No!" Jordie wailed, "I can't have a hangover. My mum will kill me at lunch tomorrow."

Emma rolled her eyes.

"You'll be fine Jordie, you didn't drink as much as some of the others. I watched you. Let's just get you to bed and you'll feel alright in the morning,"

Emma soothed, lifting Jordie's one arm and Jed lifting the other.

They managed to get Jordie to her room and as careful as possible dropped her onto her bed. Emma pulled the covers over her flatmate and wished her a good night.

Back in the living room Jed smiled sheepishly and picked up his coat and scarf from the table near the front door.

"Thanks again for your help," Emma said, not quite being able to meet his gaze. He made her uncomfortable. At first he seemed difficult, then he was almost unbearably kind. She didn't know what to make of him, nor of the strange feeling now dancing around her insides.

"My pleasure," he said, a smile lighting up his features and his head bowed slightly as he said goodnight.

Emma could barely breathe, her insides now in absolute turmoil at the briefest glance of that smile. What was happening? She asked herself. It must be the drink, she reasoned, but strangely enough she didn't feel the least bit reassured.

*　　*　　*

The First Day of Christmas.

Emma woke with a start. It was Christmas Day. It had finally arrived. All the Christmas anthems blaring out the radio for weeks on end, the packed out shops and heaving streets, the niggle of festive excitement that even as an adult Emma still happily succumbed too, all culminated in just one day in the year. And here it was.

Despite having only crawled into bed at one in the morning, Emma felt surprisingly fresh and alert and ready to make the most of the day. She was still overtired and desperately needed a longer holiday and yet that didn't seem to matter on the twenty fifth of December. Nothing else mattered for the next twenty four hours.

She made her way to the kitchen and made herself a strong coffee, leaving enough in the pot for Jordie who no doubt needed it even more than Emma did. The kitchen clock's hands showed that it was just a few minutes past eight. Emma was pleased. Despite the late night, she'd actually managed more hours sleep than she had in weeks.

As she sipped her coffee her mind drifted back to the night before. The enigma that was her new neighbour, from his moodiness at their first meeting, to the helpful and pleasant man he morphed into during the course of the party, played at her thoughts. And the way her stomach had dipped and lurched at his direct gaze bothered her more than she dared to admit, or was willing to analyse too closely.

Emma distracted herself by mentally examining the day's timetable. Relax (read: nurse Jordie's hangover) with her flatmate for a couple of hours, watching Christmas TV re-runs, before driving the hour journey down the motorway to her Mum and Dad's for Christmas lunch. Then the obligatory walk in the afternoon, followed by more food and plenty of board games to usher in the evening. She'd stay the night and be home on Boxing Day, ready to start another shift the following morning. At least she wasn't working Christmas Day this year.

Jordie made her entrance, bleary eyed and looking like she'd had better starts to the day. Emma poured and handed her a cup of still hot coffee. Jordie smiled painfully as she took a sip.

An hour later Emma rolled herself off the sofa, finally fed up of lazing around in her pyjamas in front of the telly and headed into the bedroom to dress. Shortly after, a still delicate Jordie gave a half hearted attempt of a wave goodbye, as Emma exited the flat to make her journey home to her parents.

"Happy Christmas," came a male voice behind her.

Jed was reaching the top of the flight of stairs, returning to his flat from wherever he'd graced his presence.

"Yes," she replied ineptly, momentarily caught off guard, equally by his sudden appearance and the bright red festive sweater he was wearing.

He looked down at where she was staring.

"My mum sent it for Christmas," he said, sheepishly and an awkward smile playing on his lips. "Thought I'd better wear it, seeing as she and Dad are due to visit for lunch."

"Of course," she said, returning his smile. Despite her dislike of him the day before, Emma couldn't help but admit that he did indeed seem to be a nice guy.

"Well, have a good day Emma," and with that Jed disappeared into his flat.

Emma fought down a feeling of disappointment at their short exchange. She took two steps at a time, down to the car park, eager to get her journey over with. She longed to just relax with her family and not think about anything, or anyone, else.

*   *   *

A massive lunch, Christmas crackers, a warming fireplace and glass of port later and Emma truly felt at peace. Mum and Dad sat either side of her and their collie, Rosie, lay splayed out in front of the fire. Ripped wrapping paper still littered the floor beneath the Christmas tree and Emma's presents: perfume, the obligatory Christmas socks, a book and bath salts, sat in a neat pile at the foot of the sofa where she lounged. Her parents had even treated her to a stocking, presented within minutes of her arrival. Chocolate coins, candy canes and salted pretzels had all been consumed with relish, despite the amazing Christmas lunch which had filled her stomach to bursting.

In all honestly, she didn't want Christmas Day to end; to have to return to the reality of a busy city and an even busier job. She closed her eyes and enjoyed the warmth radiating from the crackling embers and the gentle chatter between her parents.

"Do you want some more Christmas cake love?" Emma's mother asked, standing up from the comfortable sofa and making her through the open door to the kitchen.

"No Mum, I best not," Emma replied, not opening her eyes. "I think two slices is probably enough." Not to mention the cheese and crackers which had accompanied the generous sized glass of port.

"Suit yourself."

Feeling stuffed to the gills with food and drink Emma smiled fondly. Mum had always had a great ability to feed her guests and feed them well. With a sudden sleepiness catching her off guard, Emma gave her father a sympathetic smile.

"I think that's me for the evening," she explained, standing and giving him a kiss on his whiskery cheek.

"Night love," he said affectionately.

After saying goodnight to her mother, who was still busying herself in the kitchen, Emma made her way upstairs and fell exhausted onto the comfortable guest bed. Christmas was done for another year and with that brief thought she slipped into a dreamless sleep.

*   *   *

The Second Day of Christmas. Boxing Day

After eating a mountain of leftovers and feeling no less stuffed with food than the day before, Emma begrudgingly left the comfort of her parent's and headed for home. Several traffic jams and double the expected travelling time later, she arrived rather flustered at the block of flats.

The short winter day was already showing signs of giving up. The thick grey cloud masked any attempt of brightness, with the early dusk threatening to pitch up even sooner than usual. A biting cold struck Emma as she stepped out of the car and she wondered if there would be snow arriving overnight.

Jordie was there to greet Emma as she reached the top of the stairwell.

The flat door wide open, Jordie waved enthusiastically and beckoned her in.

"I've just had the best twenty four hours," she exclaimed, giving Emma a quick hug.

Emma smiled. "So, you got over the hangover pretty quickly then?"

Jordie ignored the remark and practically danced her way over to the dining table. Laying on top was an expensive looking handbag, clearly new and no doubt a Christmas present from her loaded mother. Jordie produced a small slip of paper from inside the bag.

"Well you know how Mum always organises buffet parties on Christmas evening?" Jordie barely paused for breath or to let Emma nod. "And how she always uses it as a chance to try and matchmake me with the most ridiculous guys?" Emma managed a half nod before Jordie continued.

"Well this year, she just may well have succeeded!" she exclaimed, fluttering the slip of paper in front of Emma's face. "His name is Devon and he is gorgeous. He gave me his number and I just got off the phone with him now. I know it's a bit keen, but he's really nice," she rattled off, "and we're officially going on a date on Saturday night," she squealed the last part.

Emma raised her eyebrows.

"This Saturday? In two days time?"

"Yes! Isn't it exciting?"

"Um Jordie..." she began. "That's the night of the Christmas Do. You'd promised to be my plus one, remember?"

Jordie's face fell instantly.

"Oh," her voice barely a whisper.

Emma sighed. She thought herself a good friend and didn't want to be responsible for Jordie missing an opportunity to meet Mr Right.

"Don't worry, I'll let you off the hook. It's my boss' fault he didn't book the venue in time to get it before Christmas. Whoever heard of a post-Christmas Do anyway?"

Jordie paused, letting Emma's words sink in and to make sure she wasn't mistaken, before letting out an ear-splitting squeal of delight. She threw her arms around Emma and squealed some more.

"You're the best Emma, really you are!"

"That's all right. I'd rather not go to the Do now Christmas is over, anyway. It's a good excuse to stay in and relax."

Jordie stopped jumping in excitement and stood with her arms crossed, head on one side.

"You've never needed an excuse to stay in before. After all, that's all you ever seem to do. I'd have thought you'd enjoy getting out for once."

"That's not true," Emma began, defensively, before realising that it actually was.

"Find someone else to go with you," the spark of excitement was back in Jordie's eyes.

Emma looked incredulous. "Who?"

There was a knock at the door. Jordie flounced down the hallway, like an over excited teenager and opened the door wide. Jed stood on the other side with two gifts in his hands.

"Are these for us?" Jordie exclaimed, without even greeting him first.

Yep, definitely acting like a teenage girl, Emma thought wryly.

"Sorry about my flatmate," she apologised. "She's met a guy and all good manners have flown out the window."

Jed laughed and handed the gifts over as he stepped into the room.

"That's so kind," Jordie said, totally unabashed by Emma's comments.

"Don't get too excited," Jed explained. "I was given them by friends, and seeing as I'll never get around to eating them and the five other boxes I was given this year, I wondered if you girls would like them?"

Emma looked down at the box of chocolates he offered out to her and smiled tightly. It wasn't that she didn't appreciate the gesture, but seeing as she herself had also received several boxes, she doubted she'd quickly get through all hers either.

"Thanks."

Jordie regained her manners long enough to offer Jed a glass of wine, which he duly accepted, before she steered him over to the sofa. Emma hovered for a few seconds, unsure whether she wanted to join them. He still made her feel uncomfortable for some unknown reason.

"Emma has a dilemma," she heard Jordie say. A sinking feeling crept into her gut. She could guess where this was headed.

"So," Jordie announced, having quickly explained the situation and before Emma had managed to stop her, "I was thinking that maybe you could accompany Emma to the Do?"

Emma took in a sharp breath. Jed looked embarrassed and raised his eyes to hers briefly, a look of uncertainty flickering across his features. She felt cross. What had he to feel embarrassed and unsure about? Was she really that bad, that the thought of a few hours in her presence provoked such a reaction?

"I guess I could," he said slowly. "If Emma is happy about that?"

He looked at her again, this time his expression was masked and Emma couldn't decipher whether he actually wanted to go or not.

"Of course not," she said, realising how rude it sounded only once the words were out of her mouth. "I just mean that I can't possibly expect you to do that. We barely know each other. What would your girlfriend think?"

"I don't have one," he replied, the hint of a smile on his lips.

Emma realised she'd just unwittingly asked the question that suggested she was interested in him, and how he'd recognised it too. She stuttered in embarrassment,

"I just meant that it's a bit inappropriate. You've just moved in and I don't know you at all. You could be a mentalist or something."

"Or something," he confirmed with the same playful smile.

She looked away, ill at ease with the sudden fluttering feeling in her stomach. She wished he'd stop smiling like that.

"Don't worry about it. I'm not going to go. I have to work the next day anyway, so I won't want a late night."

Jordie harrumphed and rolled her eyes. "You never just go out and have fun," she said. "Let Jed take you. You need to let your hair down a bit."

"Well, that will never happen anyway," Emma fought back. "It's a work do. They're always awkward. Besides I'll spend the entire evening being bombarded with questions about Jed as everyone will be convinced he's my boyfriend."

Just the thought of the inevitable interrogation made her feel worn out.

"Well, that's settled then," Jed said, finishing his drink and standing. "Emma's made her decision."

He looked almost relieved which both shocked and annoyed her. He really did seem to dread the thought of spending time with her. She was tempted to change her mind just to frighten him.

"Spoilsport," Jordie hissed, although it wasn't clear whom she was addressing.

"Well maybe we can go for just an hour or so," Emma said, keen to just see his startled reaction.

"Okay then," he replied, nonchalantly and she baulked as she realised that not only had she been wrong about him not wanting to go, she had now committed to taking him with her. She ignored Jordie grinning like a Cheshire cat behind him and tried to act as nonchalant as he had.

"Lovely. You can either pick me up here at seven thirty or meet me there, if you like."

"I'll be here at seven thirty," he smiled warmly and made his way to the door, waving goodbye over his shoulder.

Jordie chuckled quietly to herself as Emma quickly escaped to the kitchen under the guise of making a cup of tea.

*   *   *

The Third Day of Christmas, 27th December

The heavy blanket of night barely a chance to lift before Emma's alarm rudely pierced the sleepy air. She forced herself out of her warm and comfortable bed and shook involuntarily despite the heating being on already.

Only the occasional car along the main road punctuated the silence and Emma fought the feeling of slightly despondency she always got, thinking of most of the population still tucked up in bed. She loved her job, so the early starts and late finishes were worth it. It just didn't make leaving a toasty warm bed any easier.

An hour and a half later Emma had started her shift. Gulping down a mug of fresh coffee from the constantly topped up coffee pot in the staff kitchenette, she waited on the first patient to arrive for their blood pressure check.

Arlene stood next to her. A fully trained nurse, Arlene checked the fridge for the vaccinations she'd need that day, making sure she had the right quantity and that they were still within date. Confident that she had what she needed, Arlene picked up her half finished mug of coffee and turned her attention to Emma.

"My daughter's planning on watching back to back Christmas movies, tucked up on the sofa under a blanket all day," Arlene confessed. "While I've got a nine hour shift to look forward to. Sticking needles into strangers who hate me for it. Telling off everyone who's sent their blood sugar levels sky-rocketing by overindulging the last few days. Dealing with all the others who would really rather be anywhere else during the holiday period and are determined to take it out on me. Sounds fun doesn't it?!"

Emma laughed and nodded in agreement and solidarity.

"Well at least we've got the late Christmas Do to look forward to. I need to let my hair down," Arlene said. "Who are you bringing?"

"Well my flatmate was going to come," Emma replied reluctantly, uncomfortable with the direction of the conversation.

"So, they're not now then? You going on your own instead?"

"Um..." Emma hoped for a sudden commotion or arrival of a patient to avoid having to answer the question, but none came.

"My neighbour agreed to come instead," she said as confidently and nonchalantly as possible.

"Mrs Olban?" Arlene asked incredulously. Emma had regaled Arlene and the other staff with many fond stories of the eccentricities of her elderly neighbour.

"No, the other one," Emma replied, hiding her gaze in her coffee cup.

"Oh yes?" Arlene smiled knowingly.

Emma sighed, realising that any pretence was now futile. Arlene was a mother of a teenage daughter, Emma reasoned. There was no way anything was getting past her.

"Yes. They're new. Just moved in a few weeks ago. Jordie was meant to come, but she has a date, so the neighbour kindly offered to take her place."

"Does this new neighbour have a name?"

"Of course. Jed. I didn't catch the surname." Emma busied herself with pouring a second cup of coffee, trying to ignore Arlene's intent stare and the flush that was starting to spread across her own cheeks.

She was saved from an onslaught of questions by a smattering of patients arriving into the waiting room. Grabbing her newly filled mug, she smiled a rather smug 'goodbye' and quickly headed into her cubicle.

*   *   *

After a busy shift, during which Arlene thankfully hadn't had time to ask any more questions, Emma headed home. She looked forward to an evening in front of the TV watching Christmas re-runs. Armed with a cut-price bottle of Mulled Wine from the local supermarket, she entered the flat with a dramatic sigh of relief, mingled with contentment.

A warm glass of mulled wine later, Emma sat on the sofa feeling relaxed. A plate of Christmas lunch leftovers, that her Mum had insisted she take back with her, lay across her legs and she gratefully tucked into the feast.

Jordie was nowhere to be seen and Emma guessed she'd chosen to attend one of the many invites from her vast collection of friends. Jordie had the amazing ability to be friends with anyone of any background or personality. From hippies to smartly dressed business women, from tortured artists to trendy 'it' girls, Jordie had a penchant to befriend them all. It was no surprise that rarely a week went by without several social invitations.

Emma, on the other hand, liked to keep her friendship circles small. Jordie, Arlene and another couple of girls from work, her childhood best friends Naomi, Olivia and Jess from University were the only ones she still saw regularly. Almost absent-mindedly, she decided it was time she picked up the phone and organised a night out with some of the girls. It had been too long.

Mulled wine and leftovers finished, having watched re-runs until she was utterly bored of them, she made her way to bed. Tomorrow evening was the night of the work do and she needed a good chunk of sleep to get through the long day ahead of her. The thought of taking Jed entered her mind and she felt the, now familiar, rising heat in her cheeks. She shook it off quickly and pushed him from her mind. All that was left was a slight tinge of disappointment that she hadn't heard or seen him that day, before she allowed sleep to take over and interrupt her betraying thoughts.

*   *   *

The Fourth Day of Christmas, 28ᵗʰ December

Even the busyness of the following working day did little to distract
Emma from her growing nerves. The thought of the work do was bad
enough, but coupled with her 'date' for the evening, Emma was fast
descending into a panic.

Why had she risen to the bait and agreed to let Jed accompany her? She
barely knew him and the few conversations they'd had contained more
words spoken in irritation than any other. And why exactly did he make her
feel so nervous? Yes, he was good looking and seemed charming enough,
but he wasn't really her usual type. She just wished she'd been bold enough
to say "no" and spend the evening relaxing in front of a film instead. She'd
just have to get the evening over and done with and never make the same
mistake again.

"So, about this neighbour?" Arlene asked, as if reading her thoughts.
She'd sidled up to Emma while deep in thought and hadn't noticed.

"Is he cute?"

Emma sighed. "He's all right, but he's just a friend."

"Sometimes that's how it starts."

Emma turned to Arlene and raised her eyebrow.

"You can't take no for an answer can you? You're determined to set me
up."

Arlene smiled wickedly and patted Emma on the shoulder as she walked
away.

*   *   *

The mad dash home after work was followed by the mad dash to get
ready. Drinks were being served at eight, with a sit down dinner at nine.
Seeing as Emma had only finished her shift at six thirty and had a thirty
minute commute back home, getting ready for a night out with only half an
hour to spare before Jed arrived was a tall order.

Somehow she managed to shower, drive a brush through her out of
control end-of-the-day hair (which she was grateful she'd washed that
morning), throw on a clean sparkly dark green dress and smear a decent
amount of make up on, all before the knock at the door.

Slipping on her high heels and grabbing a sparkly clutch bag, Emma took
a deep breath trying to squash down the nerves and opened the door.

Jed stood the other side wearing a smart but casual grey-blue shirt and
pair of chinos. His heavy winter overcoat was back, as was his bright red

scarf. He looked good and Emma's nerves came flooding back.

"Hello," was all she managed and which came out far more abruptly than she'd hoped.

"Hi," he grinned, shooting an admiring glance at her appearance. She was secretly pleased by his approval, but the realisation annoyed her.

Nerves, mixed with not wanting to attend the Do, mixed with confusing thoughts toward her new neighbour all combined to make Emma feel less than jovial.

"Shall we go?" he asked.

Emma hesitated briefly before stepping out of the door and facing the evening ahead.

*   *   *

The room was dimly lit with blaring music blaring and a busy bar where the majority of Emma's work colleagues were gathered. Long tables stretched out along the opposite wall, with the place settings gleaming under twinkly Christmas lights.

"This looks nice," Jed, shouting over the music, said reassuringly.

It did not, but she appreciated the effort he was making.

Arlene came bounding over, the glint in her eye still there from earlier in the day. Emma hoped she wouldn't be too brutal.

"Hi, I'm Arlene. I work with Emma. And you?" she asked, with a side wink to Emma. Emma cringed.

"Jed," Jed replied. "I fell out with Emma over a Christmas tree. Oh, and I'm her neighbour too."

Arlene lifted an eyebrow in amusement, gave her a 'what else haven't you told me' look and proceeded to offer them a drink.

"No Arlene, I'll get my own," Emma began to protest.

"No, I'll buy you both one," Jed interjected.

"Well, what I was about to explain, but thank you for the kind gestures, is that the first drink is free, then we have to pay," Arlene rolled her eyes, clearly miffed by how cheap their boss was.

"Oh," they both said in unison and followed Arlene to the bar.

A few drinks later and the three course meal eaten (disappointingly an almost cold Christmas dinner, preceded by a hideously old fashioned prawn cocktail starter with limp lettuce, and a stodgy Christmas pudding for afters) and the majority of the Emma's colleagues were back at the bar or already dancing badly on the disco floor.

The sheer noise, plus the layout of the table, meant that Emma had barely exchanged a word with Jed other than, 'please may you pass the mustard?' She felt bad for having dragged him along and felt that the evening very much made up for his rudeness at their first meeting. She smiled apologetically in his direction and he laughed.

"I've been to worse," he shouted over the music, correctly reading her expression.

"Really? That's astonishing," she shouted back.

He grinned widely and her heart did a little flip. She quickly raised her glass to her lips, partly to hide any reaction she might have exhibited at the sudden feelings inside, but also to distract herself from the reality that she might, just might, be a little bit attracted to Jed.

"Do you want to go?" she managed to hear him ask above the thumping music.

She nodded and having said goodbye to Arlene and a few others, they quickly headed out the door. She breathed in the fresh night air and checked her watch. It was still early enough to not have to worry about being half asleep on the job the following morning.

"Do you want to grab a coffee before I get you home? Decaf?" he asked. "I know a place that's open late."

Tempted to just run home as fast as her high heels would allow (the thought of spending more time with him suddenly a daunting prospect), Emma instead found herself nodding in reply.

*   *   *

"So, tell me about yourself," she asked, after they'd both ordered their drinks; Emma a decaf chai and Jed a filter coffee.

The café was closer to a greasy spoon than a trendy coffee bar, but it was quiet and after feeling the pinch of the cost of drinks at the venue, it was gratifyingly cheap.

Emma hoped her question would negate the need to talk much herself, but to instead listen to whatever Jed had to say and use the opportunity to relax and unwind. She was exhausted. However, she found what Jed had to say very interesting. Or perhaps it was just Jed himself.

"So that's how I ended up being a professor," he concluded, having explained his choice of degree, his travels to various exotic locations and his passion upon his return to teach.

"And you enjoy what you do?" Emma asked, realising that she'd been leaning in the entire time he'd been sharing his life story.

"Yes, I do. There's something incredible in knowing that what I say has the potential to open opportunities in another's life. Of course, we all have the chance to do that. But in my profession, it can be a daily occurrence impacting multiple students. What about you? What exactly do you do?"

"Well, I always wanted to be a nurse, but I had a hard time at college and didn't make the grades to study nursing. At the time I just couldn't face repeating the year, so I went out and got whatever job I could find," Emma confided, surprised by how easy it was to open up to Jed.

"After a couple of years I was bored with dead end jobs and bored with earning a minuscule wage, so I decided to return to college. I got a placement working at the hospital while I was studying and by the time I'd finished the year, and could go on to nursing school, I'd been offered a permanent position which I accepted instead.

I love what I do at the hospital and I knew with some vocational courses, which work pays for, I could gradually increase my skills and qualifications. I may never be a fully qualified nurse, but I've already added so many strings to my bow doing things this way round."

"So, what is your job then?" Jed laughed.

"Sorry, I'm blabbering," Emma smiled apologetically.

"Not at all, I like hearing your story. I'm just curious."

"Well, I assist the nurses' with their patients and general routine stuff, like stocking up the rooms. I took vocational classes last year which allows me to take blood pressure and vitals, so I have specific appointment slots where I can see patients so nurses don't have to. I'm planning to study through work again and get the qualifications so I can take bloods. I've also trained up in the pharmacy and half my shift is spent there, putting together patient's prescriptions and ordering stock in. There's lots more I can train up for, which will increase my potential for promotion and pay rises. Plus, like you, I love what I do. Despite the crazy long shifts and rare weekends off that is!"

Emma suddenly felt uncomfortable by the way Jed was looking at her and she quickly lowered her gaze to her chai, which had just a few dregs left at the bottom.

"You make my career sound like one big holiday," she could hear the smile in his voice.

"Hardly," she protested. "Don't teachers have incredibly hectic amounts of paperwork and preparation?"

"Yes, true," he tipped his head to one side. "Just a few nights ago I seem to remember you thinking I had it easy, what with the long school breaks. I remember you being quite put out."

Emma knew he was teasing her, and the brief glimpse in his direction confirmed it, as a big grin crept across his face. She blushed with embarrassment and not just for her comments the previous evening.

"Well, I was a bit put out having been verbally attacked over the trifling matter of a Christmas tree," she replied, glad she still had some clout left in her amongst the confusing emotions she was feeling.

He laughed heartily and she couldn't help but join in. They sat smiling nervously at each other for a time, while Emma racked her brains for something to say.

"Right," he announced, breaking the silence and looking at his watch. "You're working tomorrow, aren't you? We'd better get you back."

Emma checked her watch and audibly groaned. When they'd left the venue it had only been half past ten, now it was after midnight. Had they really chatted for so long? She was surprised they hadn't been thrown out the café, which displayed their closing time as midnight.

"The Manager's a friend of mine," Jed said in explanation, when she mentioned it to Jed.

"So, I have you to blame for keeping me out so late?" she said, only half joking. She was as annoyed with herself as him. She knew she'd suffer when she had to get up for work in just four hours time.

He looked suitably bashful and apologetic as they quickly made their way across town and approached the block of flats. As they reached her door, he said a hushed "sorry" and "thanks for tonight", before giving her a peck on the cheek. The glance he gave her as he stepped away made up for the late night, as Emma felt a pang in her stomach at his endearing look.

As he stepped out of sight, into his own flat, Emma took a deep steadying breath.

*   *   *

The Fifth Day of Christmas, 29th December

The following morning at work was painful. She woke with a pounding headache through lack of sleep, and three coffees within the first ninety minutes of her shift had done little to take away the groggy spaced feeling. At least she was in good company; most of her colleagues were suffering the consequences of too much alcohol and one had even called in sick.

Also competing with Emma's limited brain power was the thought of the evening spent with Jed. She couldn't lie to herself any longer. She liked him. He was actually a great guy and not the horrible ogre she'd first imagined him out to be. And the way he'd looked at her as they parted company hinted that he possibly liked her too.

The thought hurt Emma's head and she winced. She had enough to cope with just getting through the ten hour shift, on what had ended up only being three hours sleep. She'd worry about possible crushes another time.

She also felt bad that she hadn't thanked Jed properly for coming with her and for being such a good sport. She'd enjoyed talking with him and felt it was only polite to let him know.

Hours later, dragging her tired legs up the seemingly infinite flights of stairs (the lift still hadn't been fixed), she contemplated going to thank him straight away. But sheer exhaustion, she felt, won over good manners.

She practically fell through the door into the flat and with tunnel vision began to make her way to her bedroom.

"Emma!" a voice shrieked, full of ecstatic emotion. "I have so much to tell you about my date last night!"

Emma vaguely recognised Jordie's shape in front of her, the usually sharp contours of her body looking decidedly blurry around the edges. Emma managed an 'hmm', in response to Jordie's over enthusiasm, before the room began to sway rather dramatically.

Emma, for some reason emitted another 'hmm' before Jordie disappeared completely and Emma felt herself falling out of control onto the floor.

*   *   *

The Sixth Day of Christmas, 30th December

Feverish dreams kept her tossing and turning all night. She woke a few times, only to feel her head would explode if she didn't shut her eyes again immediately. Night seemed to last forever, the intense dark foreboding and oppressive in its constant thick blanket of black.

She wanted her mum. She couldn't really remember where she was or how she'd got there. Occasionally she thought she heard voices, but never saw any faces.

Eventually a tiny sliver of light penetrated the sheet of night and when she next awoke the curtains held a greyish glare, the brightest the winter sun could manage. She was in her bed, dressed in her pyjamas and dripping with sweat. Despite her fuzzy head she recognised that she was ill and vaguely recalled dropping at Jordie's feet the night before.

Her room was empty, but a glass of water, an empty bucket, tissues, a thermometer and her mobile phone lay next to the bed. No doubt Jordie had attempted to nurse her at some point in the small wee hours.

Emma tried to reach for the phone, but her whole body ached, and she sank back under the covers.

"Emma?" came a tentative whisper through the door.

"Jordie," Emma tried to rasp back.

Jordie entered Emma's bedroom, carrying a tray with a plate of toast and cup of sweet hot tea.

"I don't know if you can manage anything to eat, but I'll leave this here for you. You haven't vomited, but you were running a fever for quite a while," Jordie explained. "I have to go to work, but Jed will come and check on you through the day."

"Jed?" Emma choked the words, partly wondering how he was involved and partly horrified of the thought of him seeing her sick in bed.

"When you collapsed last night, I couldn't lift you and I was freaking out. I didn't know what had happened. So, I ran and got Jed," Jordie said. "He was amazing. He took control of everything. Once we realised that you were okay and just sick and not dying or anything, he stayed for hours to take turns checking on you."

"He was in here?" Emma felt a blush rise up her cheeks.

"Yes. Oh, but he was very professional," laughed Jordie, upon seeing Emma's expression. "He seemed very concerned about you," she added with a knowing and mischievous look.

Emma ignored her. "My pyjamas?"

Jordie grinned in response. "Me of course. Relax. Anyway, when you're feeling better, I have to tell you about my date last night," Jordie blew a kiss and waved. "No rush of course," and she disappeared out of the room.

Emma contemplated the toast and tea, before closing her eyes and falling back to sleep.

*   *   *

Waking, just as groggy as before, Emma noticed that the breakfast had been replaced with a mug of soup. This meant that Jed must have been in the flat. She actually felt disappointed to have missed him. She managed to pull herself into a seated position, her muscles and joints complaining rather than screaming as they had that morning.

Looking back to the soup, wondering if she could reach it, she noticed a scribbled note leaning against the mug.

I'll pop in again this afternoon sometime. If you need me, call the number below. Jed

The simplicity and normality of the note was touching. She reached out for the soup and painfully reeled her arm back in, the mug gripped within her fingers. She sipped it carefully, pleased that it was both warm and her favourite flavour: chicken. It meant that Jed hadn't left that long before and she hoped it wouldn't be too long before he returned.

*   *   *

"We were worried about you," came a gentle voice.

Realising that she was still sat up in bed, Emma opened her eyes from her nap. The empty soup mug had been removed and Jed stood beside the bed with a hot beverage in his hand.

"Tea?"

"Thanks," she croaked and tried, unsuccessfully, to hide how happy she was to see him.

"I didn't want to wake you but I heard you stirring. I didn't realise that you were still asleep, sorry."

"No, it's fine. I don't think I was sleeping deeply."

Taking the proffered tea gratefully she sipped the sweet, hot drink.

"How are you feeling now?" Jed asked, sitting down on the chair next to the bed.

"Terrible, but not as bad as earlier. What about work?" Emma suddenly exclaimed as she remembered she was meant to be on shift.

"Jordie phoned and explained, so don't worry. They said to take your time and get better. Apparently, you're off tomorrow anyway."

She had been careful to book off New Years' Eve and New Years' well in advance. It would now be spent ill in bed. She sighed.

"What?"

"Nothing, I was just looking forward to my days off, that's all."

"What did you have planned?"

"Jordie and I were going to a friend's New Years' Eve party in the countryside. We were going to stay over and make a break of it."

"Sorry about that," Jed said, looking contemplatively for a moment.

"Why are you sorry?"

"Well firstly your plans have been ruined, but secondly it's all my fault."

"What are you on about?" Emma replied, shortly.

Jed gave a slight smile at her abruptness. Apparently, the virus hadn't completely sapped her defensive side.

"When we first met, I had just got over the flu. It seems I may have passed it on to you," he explained, looking remorseful.

Emma thought for a moment.

"True, but I work with sick people. Plus, it's not exactly uncommon to go down with colds and bugs, especially this time of year. I have had the flu jab though, so this might not be that."

Jed's eyebrows raised and he looked a little less guilty.

"Well I hope not. I was out for two weeks with it and I'd hate to see you go through that. Though of course, I'll be here every day to help you if you need it."

"Thanks," Emma whispered, trying to ignore the flip in her stomach at his offer. The thought of seeing him every day was quite a nice one.

*   *   *

The Seventh Day of Christmas, 31st December, New Years' Eve

25

"So, you don't mind me going on my own then?" Jordie asked for the nineteenth time.

"I've said I don't. There's no point both of us hanging around the flat feeling miserable," Emma stated, feeling just that.

"It's just such a shame that Devon can't come," Jordie said, a dreamy look descending across her features. "He's already got plans, but we are definitely going out again next week. I can't wait," she squealed excitedly.

Jordie, upon seeing Emma sitting up and half coherent the evening before, had proceeded to regale her with the full version of her first date with Devon. Cutting through all the hyperbole and attention to detail, Emma came to the quick conclusion that Jordie was crazy over the guy and sincerely hoped he felt the same about her friend. At least he'd agreed to a second date, which was a good sign.

Jordie grabbed her overnight bag from the table and hugged Emma.

"I'll see you tomorrow, hun."

"Right, see you then," Emma replied, trying to smile bravely at Jordie as she left.

Having managed to prise herself out of bed that morning, Emma spent most of the day watching films with Jordie and Jordie had kindly stocked the fridge with treats for Emma before she packed for the night away.

Still feeling delicate, but thankful that her appetite was returning, Emma shuffled her way to the fridge to decide on what to eat first. Already six in the evening, she felt she might as well start celebrating now, seeing as she was unlikely to make it to midnight.

Settling down to a pack of sushi and yet another film to pass the time, there was a knock at the door. Painfully she stood and made her way to answer it, feeling rather annoyed with whoever it was, for disturbing her unnecessarily.

"Hi," said Jed, standing with his arm on the door frame and looking rather handsome all of a sudden.

"What are you doing here?" she spluttered, rather rudely.

He smiled. "Well, I couldn't really expect a warm welcome, could I?"

"Sorry, I'm just surprised. Don't you have a party to go to?" Emma hit her forehead with her palm, before instantly regretting it. "Of course, you do. You're just here to check on me, right?"

"Wrong. Seeing as your New Years' plans have been so catastrophically ruined, I thought it only fair that you not spend it on your own."

"No," Emma said forcefully. "You can't abandon your plans because my own plans fell apart. That's ridiculous."

"Who says I have plans anyway?" came his reply.

"You don't? I find that hard to believe."

"Well, unless you count spending the evening with my younger brother, who's lamenting the recent break up of his relationship to a wannabe WAG, and his equally charming drunk friends, I think it's only right to regard that option as not being a good enough 'plan' for New Years'."

"And what about your own friends?"

"Most of them are married and are therefore attending various coupley events this evening. I'm a few years older than you. I'm the last single guy in my group of friends."

"Oh," was the only reply Emma could think of.

"So, can I come in then?"

Emma nodded which set off a coughing fit, as Jed stepped through the door. He immediately handed her a bottle of cough medicine which, in lightning speed, he'd fished out of the bag he was carrying.

"I've got everything we could possibly need in here," he said confidently, putting the bag on the table. He began pulling items out one at a time.

"Paracetamol, cough sweets, those tissues with balm-what's-it-called on them, travel scrabble, chocolate, two DVDs (one a chick flick, one action), crisps and a bottle of champagne for when the clock strikes twelve. Sorry that it's not quite up to the standard of a party in a country house."

"It's perfect, thank you," Emma said warmly, hugging her arms around herself and feeling more than a little close to tears.

"What do you feel like?" he asked, holding up the DVDs in one hand and the scrabble in the other. "Sorry it's a bit of a geeky game, but... well actually I'm not sorry, I love scrabble!"

Emma laughed. "Me too, but unfortunately my brain won't cope with it tonight. I feel like my head is swimming underwater, independent from my body. A DVD will have to do. You choose."

Jed grinned and picked the action one. Emma didn't mind. The thought of watching a chick flick with Jed seemed a bit intimate, not to mention a little weird.

The evening ticked by slowly, Emma drifting in and out of sleep as the film played. The first time she awoke, she noticed that Jed had pulled a blanket over her to keep her warm. As the credits rolled, she woke again and sat up as quickly as she was able, embarrassed to have missed so much of the film Jed had specially brought over. But he didn't seem bothered.

"Can I get you anything?" he asked, jumping up from the sofa and heading for the kitchen. Emma noted how at home he seemed and smiled to herself. There was something so comfortable and easy about spending time with Jed and yet when he looked at her, she felt a distinct shot of electricity, which wasn't comfortable in the least.

"Just water please," she croaked.

He looked around the kitchen door in her direction, a look of concern across his face.

"You can go to bed if you like, don't stay up for me. I really don't mind."

"I'm awake now, it's fine."

He returned to the sofa, handing her a glass of water, and sitting down.

"So, we've another three and a half hours to kill. We could watch the other DVD, or we could chat. Although seeing as you're not fit to talk for long, I guess I'll be the one doing all the talking."

Emma smiled apologetically.

"You can watch the DVD if you want, or any of ours. I'm not great company at the moment."

"I beg to differ. You're still far better company than my brother would have been. Even that first night we met, you were still preferable."

"Thanks," Emma said, rolling her eyes.

They sat in companionable silence for a few minutes, before Emma turned to him.

"Okay, so what do you want to know?"

*　　*　　*

She looked up at the clock in surprise, when after what had felt like a half hour of talking, Jed had jumped up from the sofa and exclaimed "It's time!"

She couldn't quite believe what she saw; the long hand creeping dangerously close to join the short hand at the top of the clock face. It was five to twelve. She was stunned to think that not only had they talked for such a length of time, but that she'd managed to make it to midnight at all. Her strength bolstered slightly at the revelation, she gladly accepted the glass of champagne from Jed. She'd worry about how it might affect her afterwards.

Switching the TV back on, they turned their attention to the screen, as the news reporter enthusiastically prepared the viewers for the countdown. As the chimes began to sound, Emma sneaked a look in Jed's direction just as he turned to her. For a brief moment their eyes met and Emma felt like she couldn't breathe.

He smiled with a little uncertainty and then an unmistakable glimmer of hope passed across his features. She quickly looked away. She quietly berated herself as she did, wishing she could have been bolder and not allowed fear to creep in. But now the moment was lost and she wanted to kick herself for being so stupid.

Jed had already turned his attention back to the TV, showing no obvious signs that he was unhappy. Emma tried to concentrate on the remainder of the countdown. It seemed to go on forever. Finally, the last chime sounded and the TV erupted in a myriad of screaming crowds, fireworks and around the world scenes.

Jed raised his glass to hers.

"Happy New Year!" he exclaimed and gave her a slightly awkward side hug.

It was obvious he didn't want to overstep his boundaries and Emma hugged him back, inwardly sighing at her earlier reluctance.

*   *   *

The Eighth Day of Christmas, 1st January, New Years' Day

Emma woke to the peace of a near empty flat. No radio blaring or noises of breakfast being prepared. No water pipe rattling with the pressure of the shower head, or the sound of wardrobe doors being slammed carelessly. The only discernible noise was the slight rustle of covers as she stretched out comfortably.

Reaching one arm out for her mobile, resting on the bedside table, she took a look at the time. It was already ten in the morning. But then she only got to bed in the early hours, having said goodbye to Jed shortly after they'd finished watching the TV show and had attempted a bad rendition of Auld Lang Syne, which had inevitably ended in giggles.

Pleased that she'd still managed to have a decent night sleep she settled back against her pillow with a happy sigh. She was feeling far better than the previous two days, but the tell tale symptoms of a heavy cold still lingered. Fortunately, the blocked nose and scratchy throat hadn't kept her awake half the night.

As she closed her eyes and breathed in the peaceful atmosphere, the familiar beep of her phone announced a new message. Reaching out her arm again, this time more reluctantly, she pulled her phone closer.

Feeling up to a little trip? Jed

Emma sat up startled. She didn't even know where Jed had got her number from and the sudden appearance of his message on her phone sent her heart racing. She reprimanded herself. She really needed to get a grip over this guy. Jed was great, but she hated feeling like an animal in headlights around him.

Forcing herself out of bed she headed for the shower. She needed time to think on her response.

*   *   *

A bit better. Depends what you have in mind.

Pitifully it was the best she was able to come up with. She busied herself with making brunch, keeping one ear open for another beep signalling a reply. None came, so she sat down to eat, feeling rather fed up.

The knock at the door spurred her into action, abandoning her food in an instant and making her way to the door in record time. She tried to take a calming breath before opening the door, but it didn't seem to make much difference to her rapidly beating heart.

"Morning," Jed grinned, as she unlocked the catch and pulled the door toward her. "You look much better today."

"I am. A bit," Emma managed, completely ineptly. She was still trying to deal with the impact his smile had on her insides.

"Well if you're up for it, I've got to go out and help out a friend. Do you want to come?"

It didn't sound too appealing, if Emma was honest, and she shrugged non-committedly.

"What exactly does that entail?"

He laughed at her unimpressed expression.

"Don't worry, you won't be changing a tyre or mucking out horses or anything like that. I just promised some friends I'd feed and walk their dog today. They're visiting family for New Years' Day and the father-in-law is allergic to dog hairs apparently. So, they couldn't take the dog with them and pulled in a favour."

"Oh, well why didn't you just say. I love dogs."

"Good, then get your coat."

*   *   *

A fifteen minute drive later and Emma was amazed to find that they had travelled out of town and into what looked like a little hamlet surrounded by fields and cows.

"I didn't even think you could get countryside this close by," she gasped as Jed drove them down a narrow lane.

"Pretty incredible isn't it? What I'd do to be able to afford a property out here."

Emma sighed in agreement and watched out the window with an almost childlike fascination. To think that Jordie had faced a three hour commute to reach her countryside destination, without either of them realising how much closer the countryside actually was. She vowed to return here as often as possible.

They pulled into an even narrower lane and soon came upon an ivy-strewn wall with a black iron gate. The house beyond wasn't huge but was certainly grand looking and Emma looked at Jed in amazement.

"You're a dark horse. Friend of the rich and famous, are we?!"

"Hardly," he grinned. "They just bought it a long time ago, before the property bubble."

"Still, it's a pretty impressive property for most people."

"Wait until you see inside."

It wasn't long before she did and Jed was right, it was even more impressive than the outside. Beautifully restored wooden panelling stretched across the bottom half of each wall downstairs, with the top halves adorned with luxurious wallpaper in various exquisite designs.

A large farmhouse kitchen made up almost the entire back of the house, with a working Aga nestled into a massive fireplace. More fireplaces were found in the living room and upstairs in each of the three bedrooms. The original wooden flooring was complimented with beautifully woven rugs and thick, expensive looking, curtains matched each room's décor. Other original features included intricate cornicing and hand painted doorknobs throughout.

Realising she had yet to meet the dog, having been so engrossed by the stunning house, Emma made her way back downstairs rather sheepishly.

Jed was in the utility room off the kitchen, feeding what looked like a massive ball of wool.

"You decided to join us then?"

"Sorry, I got a bit distracted. This house is unbelievable."

Jed laughed and held out his hand toward the mutt that was fast devouring the contents of its bowl.

"This is Harry," he said.

"He's very hairy," Emma said, for want of something better to say.

"He's a Tibetan Terrier. Their coat can get quite long and he is definitely due a clip. Funny thing is they're a better breed for allergy sufferers, so I think the father-in-law is milking it a bit."

"I didn't realise you knew so much about dogs," Emma teased.

"I don't. But I googled the breed before we came. Nothing like being prepared," Jed joked with a glint in his eye.

Emma smiled self-consciously as he made eye contact.

"We'll take him for a walk after his food, if you're feeling up to it," Jed said, apparently not noticing her unease.

"Sure," she replied quickly.

*   *   *

The ground was crisp beneath their booted feet and Emma was glad she'd brought her warmest clothes. Her winter coat was buttoned up around her and her scarf, hat and gloves were pulled on tightly to try and escape the chill. What had started off a fairly mild morning was fast becoming a winter freeze.

Jed shot her frequent looks and she knew he was concerned given the cold and her recent health.

"I'm fine," she stated when he looked again.

"Five more minutes," he stated back. "I can take Harry out again a bit later if necessary."

Emma quite liked his no nonsense tone and the fact that he was taking charge.

Harry was chasing ahead, in and out of bushes and sticking his nose down random holes. He was in his element and Emma watched him amused. All of a sudden he lifted his head, stared at them, and came bolting full pelt across the terrain toward them.

He reached Emma's legs, then more like a cat than a dog, rubbed his long coat up against her. She laughed and reached down to pet his ears. The sudden action caused a coughing fit and she found herself doubled over. Harry ran off in fright and Jed helped her back upright again. It took a full minute to recover and Jed was furious.

"I'm an idiot. I should never have taken you out in this cold," he ranted to himself, despite her insistence that she was okay. "We need to get back to the house now, and you mustn't leave it again until it's time to go home."

"Yes Sir," she said jokingly.

"I'm not kidding Emma. You're sick and you're not going to get better traipsing around the freezing countryside. I should never have suggested it."

They managed to reach the house quickly, with Jed strolling ahead at a pace Emma struggled to keep up with. He flung open the door and headed straight for the living room and the fireplace there.

A wood burning stove had been installed within the cavity and a pile of dry logs sat invitingly next to it. Jed busied himself making a fire while Emma entered the room and hovered behind him.

"You can't make a fire," she squeaked.

"Yes, I can. I'm pretty good at making fires actually," he said gruffly, his attitude reminding her strongly of their first encounter over the Christmas tree. "You need to warm up."

"I mean that you shouldn't make a fire in a house where the owners are away. It's dangerous. I'll just have a bath when I get home," Emma protested.

"I'm only going to make a small one, just large enough to warm you up and then put itself out within an hour or so. Then I'll remove whatever is left inside and douse it in a bucket of water," he turned to her and managed a small grin. "I told you I knew what I was doing."

Emma sat down and watched as Jed got the fire under way. She could see the tension in his shoulders as he worked and was touched that he cared so much for her well being. Feeling another coughing fit coming on she tried to hide it, but soon caught Jed's notice.

"Let me get you a drink of water," he said, marching to the kitchen. "Do you need anything else?"

"I'm fine," she called, embarrassed but equally pleased by his attentive nature.

"Here," he said, handing her the glass of water. He sat down beside her, a concerned look upon his face. She took a sip, more to placate him than anything else. Emma looked up at him from behind the glass and saw his intense gaze.

"Jed..." she began, before they were suddenly interrupted by a frantic barking outside.

Out of the large bay window they could see the top of a moving car, which seconds later came to a stop near the front door.

"Ken and Niamh must be back already," Jed exclaimed and headed out of the living room.

Emma hovered nervously, not knowing if she was ready to meet these friends of Jed's and whether they'd be pleased to see her, a complete stranger, in their home.

Jed had obviously explained the situation, so when they entered the room, they were extremely friendly and not the least bit surprised to meet her. Emma relaxed slightly but the urge to go home grew. The cold and the coughing fits had reminded her that she wasn't well and with work to face the following morning, she wanted nothing more than to be tucked up into a warm bed where she could sleep the rest of the day and night away.

It wasn't long after that they were headed home in Jed's car. She slumped her head against the window and eyes heavy she began to drift off. Head foggy, she was only vaguely aware of their arrival at the flat. She felt Jed lift her from the seat and half hold, half carry her to the lift, which was thankfully now working. Her memory was a haze after that, but the one memory stuck with her as she fell asleep in bed, a big smile on her face; Jed kissing her on the forehead tenderly, before leaving her to settle for the night.

*   *   *

The Ninth Day of Christmas, 2nd of January.

Despite not feeling one hundred percent, Emma made it into work that morning. A decent night sleep helped bolster her for the long shift ahead and she was glad that over half of it would be spent in the relative peace and quiet of doing the pharmacy stock take.

"Are you sure you're fit enough to be back at work?" Arlene probed when Emma reached the staff room.

"Probably not," Emma sighed.

"Then what are you doing here?"

It was a good question that Emma didn't want to have to answer. The reality was she was nervous to hang around the flat in case Jed decided to visit again. Her feelings for him were growing fast. She had still yet to figure out what she wanted to happen between them. She liked him a lot, but the thought of a relationship was a daunting one. It had been so long since she'd dated anyone, that her confidence had been knocked and she already knew that she liked Jed too much to take a risk and mess it up.

The day progressed slowly, but Emma managed through and eventually headed out into the cold night air for the commute home. As she arrived at the flats, she felt a few flutters on her cheek and in her hair. Through the inky black sky a cascade of snowflakes descended to the earth below.

She stood in wonder, watching silently as the snow storm began to swirl and pick up pace. It was already laying as she grinned and held out her hand. The slight sting of icy water tickled her palm as the snowflakes quickly melted against the warmth of skin. She stood still for several minutes enjoying the atmosphere.

Reluctantly she turned to head indoors, to be faced with an amused looking Jed, standing just a few metres away. His arms were crossed across his thick coat and his head was tilted to one side, a smile upon his face.

"You get everywhere," she said wryly.

"Well, I guess I found the only other person in the whole building who loves the snow," he shrugged.

"Well I don't love it enough to risk getting sick again. I'm going indoors."

"That's a pity, you look really cute in the snow."

Emma blushed despite the cold. Jed's grin grew wider.

"What, even with a nose full of snot?" she couldn't help herself, using humour to deflect the feelings stirring inside.

Jed laughed uproariously. "You never can take a compliment from me."

She smiled tightly, knowing his comment to be true.

"Jordie's upstairs. She's been desperate for you to come home so she can tell you all about New Years'. I don't think I was the captive audience she was hoping for."

"Thanks for the warning."

"Emma..." she had stepped away from him to walk into the building. "Are you feeling any better? I was worried about you after yesterday."

"I've been better, but I've definitely been worse too," she was so touched by his concern that she wanted to cry.

Instead she gave him a warm smile and walked away.

*   *   *

"You would not believe the New Years' I've just had," Jordie exclaimed, the moment Emma opened the door.

"Yeah?" Emma responded, placing her bag on the floor and removing her coat.

"Well, it was all going so badly to begin with. I knew hardly anyone at the party and was missing you not being there. How are you now, anyway? Then I got this phone call, which I almost missed as it was so loud in the room, and would you believe it?" Jordie rattled off. "It was Devon! He decided that he'd rather spend New Years' with me and cancelled his plans, then drove all the way over to the party. Can you believe a guy would do that?!"

Emma shook her head, but her mind betrayed her with the briefest thought of Jed and how he probably would have.

"That's amazing Jordie. He must really like you," she replied, as she popped into the kitchen to take out a carton of soup from the fridge.

"Oh, and I'm feeling a bit better," she added, her head bobbing around the door frame.

"I really think this could be the real thing," Jordie sighed happily. "When he finally arrived, we chatted for ages, well past midnight. And, when the chimes ended and everyone was singing, he took my hands in his, looked me in the eyes and kissed me! It was so amazing."

Emma felt a stab of jealousy, but hid it as she busied herself by warming the soup in the pan.

"So, the next morning, over breakfast he asks me out on another date. Of course, I said yes! Then we walked through the gardens there and he told me how beautiful I was and we held hands for a while. Then he kissed me again. I can't tell you how hard it was to say goodbye later on. And how even harder it's been not to text him every half an hour since! Oh Emma, he is just so perfect," Jordie sighed again, and collapsed over-dramatically on the couch.

"I'm happy for you Jordie," which Emma was, but it didn't make her feel any better about her situation with Jed. Despite their growing closeness, he hadn't tried to kiss her yet.

Perhaps he had sensed her hesitation, she thought to herself, and didn't know whether to precede or not. She wasn't entirely sure how she would react if he did try and kiss her, nor whether there was any future between them. She wished she was more confident like Jordie, who seized an opportunity when it presented itself.

Instead Emma worried that she'd allowed the situation to stagnate, risking whatever feelings he may possess for her to fizzle out. But at the same time, she didn't want to be the first one to make a move. Perhaps it was old fashioned, but Emma expected Jed to, at the very least, give a clear indication that he was interested, if to not actually ask her on a date himself.

She stirred the soup too vigorously and it spilt over the side, splattering her hand. She shook it and bit her lip to the rising emotion within her. Knowing that she was still ill, it was easy to pass off the developing tears as a result of being sick, but she recognised the real reasons beneath her turmoil. Either something would have to happen with Jed, and soon, or she needed to put him out of her mind and move on.

*   *   *

The Tenth Day of Christmas, 3rd of January

Emma stared at the Christmas tree with her head on one side. With the busyness of the holidays it had become rather neglected and now hung at a slight angle, with its needles already browning. She couldn't actually remember when she'd last poured water into the bucket holding it up.

Resignedly she decided to remove the tree from the flat, eliminating the last sign of the festive season with it. Getting rid of the tree, packing away the decorations and finishing the last of the leftovers was always a depressing experience; serving as a reminder that the build up and excitement of Christmas lasted but a few days and was over for another year.

Finally feeling better after the flu, Emma was determined to hoist the offending tree out of the building by herself. She resisted the urge to call on Jed to help. She still wasn't sure how she wanted to address the situation between them and was therefore trying to keep a low profile. Besides, she'd managed to get the tree into the flat in the first place and could manage perfectly well to get it out again.

She manoeuvred the heavy object toward the kitchen, where she spent a full ten minutes trying to heave the thing out of the bucket. Needles showered onto the linoleum, sprinkling remnants of dirty water along with it. Emma struggled to get the tree into her arms and comfortably across the one shoulder, before realising the front door was still closed and she had no free hands to open it.

Sighing in frustration she dropped the tree, causing another cascade of needles, and opened the door as wide as it would go. She picked up the tree again and swayed dangerously until regaining balance. Stumbling across the hall, thanking God for the now working lift, she pressed the button with her elbow. Waiting, the tree became heavier with each second, and she vowed next year to buy a plastic one no matter how lacking in festivity it seemed.

The trip downstairs was made easier by the lift and Emma grappled bravely with the last dozen or so metres to the exit. Beyond were the industrial sized bins, already overflowing from excess rubbish from the Christmas period. Emma tucked the tree as neatly as she could against the nearest bin and spent a couple of minutes wedging it as tightly as possible, so as to avoid it toppling over onto the street. Satisfied, she turned her back to the tree and returned indoors to the warmth.

A trail of needles led her to the flat and she smiled at the memory of Christmas Eve, which now seemed so long ago. A lot had happened in a week and a half. She kept smiling as she swept up the needles, remembering again her first irate encounter with Jed. Then, his sudden appearance at their Christmas party, which had resulted in a jolt of attraction that had left her stunned.

The gradual development of their friendship over the following week and a half had made way for a deepening of feelings. Feelings she hadn't felt for anyone in a long time. As she reminisced, she realised that she did indeed want something to happen with Jed. He was fast becoming her closest friend and someone who's company she preferred over most others.

It was a startling revelation and yet it made perfect sense to her. Despite having known him only a short while, Jed had seeped into her being and Emma couldn't imagine him not being a part of her life and just the handsome and friendly guy from next door.

She re-entered the flat numbed by the realisation, but optimistic about what could happen next. She just wished she knew how to progress from where they were, as friends, to where she wanted them to be.

*   *   *

The Eleventh Day of Christmas, 4th of January

"I hate New Years' resolutions," Jordie exclaimed with a sigh, sitting down heavily at the dinner table.

"Why do you make them then?" Emma asked absentmindedly, as she tried to concentrate on filling in forms for a short pharmaceutical course.

"To better myself," Jordie pouted.

"I think that only works if you actually stick with them."

Jordie pouted some more and dropped her gym bag onto the floor beneath her.

"It just gets so difficult and boring after a while."

"It's only been three days," Emma laughed, putting her pen down and giving up trying to complete the form whilst Jordie was around.

"Well, I'm not the only one. Jed wasn't out for his run this morning like he was the first couple of days," Jordie stated, with an air of defiance.

Emma's heart did a little leap at the mention of his name and she quickly suppressed the nerves that began to stir. She hadn't seen him since the snow had fallen the evening before last. She was beginning to miss him and had more than once felt tempted to knock on his door just to see him again. The thought of scaring him off stopped her, but the disappointment of not going through with it had lingered.

"I'm seeing Devon tonight," Jordie interrupted Emma's thoughts. "What do you think I should wear?"

"Um..." Emma struggled to bring herself back to the present. "I guess it depends on where you're going."

"Out for a meal," Jordie smiled. "It sounds like a fancy place. I haven't been anywhere like that for a long time."

"Well, you should definitely dress up then. You've got loads of nice dresses," Emma felt a sudden pang, wishing she was going out for an official date with Jed and could dress up nicely for the occasion.

She mentally shook herself. Being envious of her friend's happiness and apparent success at dating wasn't going to help her own situation. Only action would do that and she couldn't sit around waiting for Jed to do all the work.

"I... I need to go out for a bit," Emma said, standing and nervously straightening her clothes.

Jordie looked up in surprise, raising her eyebrows but not saying anything. Emma opened the front door and, hesitating just briefly, made her way to Jed's flat. Her fist hovered in the air for a few seconds before connecting with his front door.

Time seemed to elapse slowly as she awaited an answer and her pulse began to race. Don't be ridiculous, she rebuked herself, I'm perfectly able to start a conversation with a guy that I like. Nothing has to come of it if I change my mind.

The click of the lock opening broke her reverie. Jed appeared and for a moment she was momentarily mute. He grinned in welcome and she felt reassured. He was ultimately and first of all her friend and she had nothing to afraid of.

"Emma."

The way he said her name threatened that thought and she took a deep breath.

"Hi Jed," she began. "I was just wondering how things are going?"

"I should be asking you that," he replied, ushering her in. "I feel terrible knowing how sick you were and that I haven't been in contact. I've just got back from a difficult family situation and I wasn't able to call."

She followed him into his flat, nervous but curious to know what his flat look liked and equally to find out what had happened. The space was surprisingly modern, especially compared to her and Jordie's place. The living room was adorned with trinkets and mementos from his travels, including pieces of furniture and art work. The plain walls acted as a canvas for the tasteful artefacts and she found she liked it.

"Um... that's okay," she remembered her manners. "I hope your family is all right. Nothing serious?"

He sighed and contemplated her for a brief moment. "I guess you'll find out soon enough. My mum has been sick for a while and she's had a bit of a relapse. I got the call just after I saw you the other evening and I headed straight there. I guess my dad could have handled it without me, but I felt I should be with them."

"I'm sorry," her voice barely above a whisper.

He stood, arms folded, in the alcove between the kitchen and the living area. He looked tired. She just wanted to hug him. Weighing up the risks of whether to take that step or not didn't seem appropriate at that moment. Someone she cared about needed comforting and that's all that mattered.

She moved forward and without making eye contact slipped her arms around his waist and leant in. His soft gasp of surprise didn't go unnoticed and she hid her embarrassment by pulling him closer. They stood for several minutes. He moved his hand to the back of her head, which was resting on his shoulder, and murmured a 'thank you' into her hair.

She wanted nothing more than to kiss him in that moment, yet something held her back. She knew that this wasn't the time. Right now, he needed her friendship above all else.

*　　*　　*

"My treat," she insisted, as they chose a table near the window. She buried her head in the menu deciding which variant of coffee was preferable. The café was abuzz with commuters, all grabbing their takeaway beverages before making the dash to the office.

A few, like Emma and Jed, were going at a slower pace and had chosen tables to sit at and sip at their purchases. With Jed not yet back at work and Emma enjoying a late start for once, it was a pleasant way to pass some time together. If it wasn't for the white elephant in the room.

Their hug back at the flat had given way to an awkward silence and a lingering, meaningful look between them. Emma had suggested grabbing a drink at the café, more to break the sudden tension in the air between them, than actually wanting a coffee.

Now she sat, menus creating a barrier between them, while she dealt with the inner turmoil inside. With Jed's news of his sick mother, she no longer knew if it was appropriate to raise the issue of their burgeoning relationship; or if there even was one. She decided to play it safe, to keep the conversation on neutral ground.

"What are you going to have to drink?"

Jed lifted his gaze from his own menu, "Espresso for me thanks, I only got back in the early hours and I didn't get much sleep."

Emma nodded, smiled sympathetically, and went to order their drinks. Returning a few moments later with Jed's espresso and her cappuccino, she joined him once again in companionable silence.

"Will your mum be okay?" she eventually asked, feeling guilty for allowing her thoughts of their relationship overshadow the seriousness of his mother's health.

"She probably will this time. But at some point, she'll get weaker and won't be able to fight it so well."

Emma sipped her cappuccino and without even thinking about it, reached across the table and took Jed's hand in hers.

"I'm sorry," she expressed, sad for Jed and his family and for what they must be going through.

He looked down at her hand over his and lifted his gaze back to hers. A jolt of electricity seemed to jump between them and she was suddenly very aware of their close proximity. She removed her fingers as casually as she could and returned her attention to the cappuccino, a shyness gripping her.

"Emma..." Jed reached out and took her fingers back in his. "It's okay."

They sat quietly for the remainder of their drinks, occasionally exchanging glances and smiles.

*   *   *

The Twelfth Day of Christmas, 5th of January

Emma woke to a blizzard. Heavy snow drifts had settled over the night time hours and a world of white welcomed those brave enough to venture out. Emma lay in bed and watched, out the window, the myriad of swirls descending peacefully through the light grey air.

Today was her day off and she felt a childlike excitement to spend it in the snow. But another huge part of her wanted nothing more than to walk over to Jed's and spend the day with him.

After the coffee the previous morning they'd walked home through the park. Jed had begun to brighten up, having shared his mother's history with her illness, and even managed to make Emma laugh with a couple of bad jokes.

Returning home, they had said a tentative goodbye. Emma had needed to get ready for work and despite the desire to continue their pleasant morning, the clock was ticking. Jed looked as if he'd wanted to say something as she announced her necessary departure, and she'd hesitated briefly at the door.

"I'd like to take you out sometime," he'd said, as she hovered with the key in the lock.

"Sure," she'd choked out.

Now she lay in bed, the new day full of promise, and smiled to herself. While the actual words hadn't been said, she now felt confident that Jed liked her. She didn't want to waste any more time circling the issue. Life was too short. His mother's illness and Jordie's enthusiasm to grab hold of opportunities had proven that to Emma. She was fed up of putting her life on hold, for work, long hours, or for any other reason.

She showered and dressed and left the comfort of her flat a short while later. Jed was exiting his flat at the same time and approached with a look of amusement of his face.

"I was coming to ask if you wanted to go play in the snow?"

Emma stifled a laugh, "and what exactly do you mean by that?"
"That did sound rather ambiguous didn't it?" Jed grinned and raised an eyebrow. "I just know that you love the snow as much as I do. It would be a shame to miss out, it'll probably be gone again tomorrow."

Emma grinned, and linking her arm in his, they made their way out of the block of flats and onto the street below.

The snow had eased slightly and crunching through the wet and cold blanket beneath their feet, they ventured out towards the common. A few children played happily; having only been back at school a few days, they were enjoying the extra unexpected day off. Emma smiled to herself, remembering Jed's comment upstairs. They really were just like big kids, going out to play in the snow, like the small children running around near them.

Jed confirmed that thought by stopping suddenly and bending down to make the torso of a snowman. Emma laughed and joined him. Soon they had a fully fledged character taking form; the sticks for arms, stones for eyes and a nose, leaves for hair. It was silly and childish, but Emma really hadn't had that much fun in a long time. And it was all thanks to Jed.

She looked up at him, all shyness forgotten, and stared at him as he worked hard to compact the last of the snowman's head. It took him a minute to realise she'd paused and his eyes met hers.

"You know I've known you less than two weeks," she said. "Yet, I've had more fun with you in just days, than I have in years."

"Well, I am a very fun guy," his eyes danced playfully.

"I'm serious Jed," she replied, feeling just that. Teasing sometimes needed to give way to the importance of a situation.

He stood up, a sudden flicker of uncertainty crossing his features. Emma started, wondering if she'd got him all wrong and had misjudged his feelings.

"Have I said something wrong?" he asked, and Emma relaxed, reassured.

"No," she whispered.

He stepped up to her and looked down directly into her eyes. His hand hovered a second, before his fingers lightly touched her cheek.

"What is it Emma?" he said, his own voice also dropping to a whisper.

She took a deep breath, "I just thought... um... I just...." her words dropped off as she realised that she didn't know what she wanted to say.

"Um...." she began again, and Jed stepped closer still. Taking her head between his hands, he grinned from ear to ear, and slowly lowered his lips to hers.

They stood there for quite a while, ignoring the children's laughter and cat calls, even ignoring the snow that had begun to swirl to the ground once again. Emma didn't care that her feet were wet and freezing and her hair was covered in the snow that had fallen off Jed's gloves. In that moment she didn't care about anything else but the two of them.

As he reluctantly pulled away, they grinned at each other and Jed laughed out loud.

"What?" Emma asked, puzzled.

"I guess I'm surprised," he confessed with a shrug of the shoulders. "Every time I've wanted to ask you out or kiss you, which has been a lot I can tell you, all I could remember was that Christmas tree and our first meeting. You seemed to hate me that evening. Okay, so that hate faded pretty quickly; you obviously now consider me a friend, but I was never quite sure if you liked me beyond that."

"So how did you know to kiss me now?"

"When you hugged me yesterday, I knew. You hadn't initiated anything up until that point. Your emotions were always so guarded. But yesterday changed that. Not to mention your sudden shyness since, which pretty much confirmed it," he grinned, a playful tone to his voice.

Emma failed to feel embarrassed by his assessment of her, knowing him to be right anyway, and leaned in for another kiss.

A few minutes later, they walked on hand in hand, and Emma smiled inwardly, thrilled by the development in their relationship and all the promise that lay therein. Jed caught her eye from time to time and she felt her heart swell.

The snow continued to fall throughout the daylight hours. As night fell the streets were silent, save the odd car slushing its tyres through the whitewashed tarmac. Lights were visible in nearly every dwelling and few creatures, great or small, dared to venture out into the chill, preferring to stay in the warm with their loved ones.

Christmas was over and done. The New Year stretched out far ahead. And the twelfth night of Christmas had reached its conclusion on the eve of its Epiphany.

The Heart of Christmas

'Twas the night before Christmas, when all through the house
Not a creature was stirring, not even a mouse;
The stockings were hung by the chimney with care,
In hopes that St. Nicholas soon would be there....'

'Who is St. Nicholas, Auntie Emma?' interrupted a little voice, the head of whom could barely be seen over the pages of the book.

'Father Christmas. Santa Claus,' Emma whispered into the small girl's strawberry blonde hair. She heard her niece gasp with excitement at the mention of the man she hoped would bring her gifts by morning.

Emma carried on reading. Ava, her three year old niece, cradled in her arms, on the bed where she was to attempt sleep, amid the thrill of Christmas Eve. Ava held her bunny close, a toy which had followed her from the cot and accompanied her everywhere. Bunny would certainly not be allowed to miss out on the big day. Or rather the two big days coming up.

Maddie watched from the bedroom door quietly, not wanting to interrupt the rare moment her sister had to bond with the little girl. Months had passed since their last visit. Maddie still felt guilty about it, especially with all the recent opportunities surrounding the wedding plans. But Maddie was familiar with feeling guilty, so she merely added it to the list.

Being back at her parent's house was an equally anxious and reassuring experience. Anxious at the feelings of failure as she faced the family, yet reassurance that she was somewhere homely, familiar and safe.

Maddie shook the thoughts from her mind as they bubbled up and threatened to pull her under, back down into self pity. She had promised not to go there. Not with Ava's first Christmas day without her father present, nor with Emma's impending wedding day. This was meant to be a happy time and the last four months had had enough sorrow to contend with.

'He sprang to his sleigh, to his team gave a whistle,
And away they all flew like the down of a thistle.
But I heard him exclaim, ere he drove out of sight -
'Happy Christmas to all, and to all a good night!''

Ava giggled loudly and clapped her hands as Emma closed the book. She turned, seeing her mother and shouted, 'Mummy' with abandoned joy. The simple and innocent display pulled on Maddie's heart strings as she accepted her young daughter's embrace.

'I hope you're going to be able to sleep tonight,' she said, laughing as she picked Ava up.

'That'll be my fault,' Emma said, as she smiled and stood up from the bed, stretching her arms tiredly. 'Three stories and a Christmas poem. I was hoping it would settle her, but I think it may have backfired.'

Maddie laughed and shook her head. 'It's her first proper Christmas, she's excited beyond reason anyway. The thought of presents waiting in the morning is too much.'

'Yes Mummy, all for me,' Ava beamed.

'Not all, some. Remember Christmas is for all of us,' Maddie gently reminded.

'Daddy too?' Ava looked confused and Maddie felt a wave of alarm.

'Umm,' Emma hovered uncertainly, amid the sudden tension in the room. 'Is it too late for some hot chocolate?'

Maddie sighed deeply. Her sister had yet to learn the danger of feeding a child sugar before bedtime, but appreciated her attempt to distract Ava. 'Go on then. Just a small cup. I doubt she'll be able to sleep for a while anyway.'

They headed downstairs together and entered the kitchen. The smells that emanated through the open door were simply magical. A generous waft of cinnamon and nutmeg, mingled with vanilla, danced in the air. Slices of ginger and orange peel were stacked in small piles on a chopping board, adding to the festive aroma. A bowl of cookie dough was being prepared by their mother. Escaped flour and blobs of butter decorated the surface below her.

'Oh, Ava, you're still awake,' Angela panicked, looking flustered amongst the steam of the kitchen. 'I was hoping she wouldn't see these until morning,' she added in a theatrical whisper to Maddie.

'It's not obvious what it's going to be yet, so don't worry,' Emma, always the problem solver, looked into the bowl at the yet uncompleted gingerbread mixture.

'We'll go to the living room while Auntie Emma fixes up the hot chocolate she promised,' Maddie smiled triumphantly, leading her daughter away from the chaos that was her mother's Christmas baking. Why Angela left it all for Christmas Eve, Maddie could never understand. It had happened every year growing up and clearly nothing had changed.

In the living room she found her father, watching some Christmas special with the dog draped over his lap. He smiled as they entered the room before turning his attention back to the TV. Ava glanced at the Christmas tree and gave a gasp of joy at the twinkling trail of lights, which lit up the delicate decorations hanging from the branches. It wasn't the first time Ava had seen it, but the excitement was afresh with each viewing. The little girl sat at the bottom of the tree and sighed happily, watching with fascination.

Maddie joined her father on the sofa, keen to finally put her feet up. She hadn't stopped since arriving at the family home that afternoon. Angela had kept the tree bare so Ava could help decorate it upon arrival, but had become quickly distracted with wedding duties with Emma, leaving Maddie to do most of the work. She hadn't minded, enjoying the bonding time with her only child.

After a quick snack for dinner, consisting mostly of mince pies and scraps of cold meats and cheeses, to make room in the fridge for the Christmas food, Maddie spent early evening bathing Ava and wrapping the last of the presents she'd brought. She looked forward to sitting in front of the TV and not having to do anything else.

*   *   *

'How are you feeling about the wedding?' Angela probed her younger daughter.

Emma was busy whisking sugar, cocoa and warm milk into a paste and trying to stay out of her mother's way. Angela got frazzled when baking and it was best to give her a wide berth.

'Oh,' Emma replied, surprised by the question. 'I feel great actually. I can't wait to be married to Jed.' It was true. She had been waiting for this day for months, following his proposal on Valentine's Day, just after their second anniversary. The thought of calling herself his wife gave her a thrill.

'That's good. So many brides get cold feet just before,' Angela stated as a matter of fact, though Emma could tell she was still probing.

'It's all right Mum. Sure, I'm nervous of the actual day; what might go wrong, or get forgotten. But marrying Jed? No, that I'm one hundred percent sure of.'

Angela nodded, but Emma couldn't discern if the answer had reassured her mother or not. 'You don't have doubts... do you Mum?'

'Oh no, he's perfect for you,' Angela waved dismissively. 'I just wondered how you were feeling. A mother's prerogative to ask.'

Emma picked up the freshly boiled kettle and finished making the hot chocolates. Her mind, for the last few weeks, had been consumed with wedding plans. So much so, that three days before the big day she decided to focus instead on Christmas. More for the break than the festivities themselves; although this time of year was always special, as it was when she and Jed had first met. She felt a flip of anticipation at the thought of Jed and his father joining them for Christmas lunch the next day. Just forty eight hours would then separate them from saying their vows.

She gave a little cough in an attempt to dislodge the thoughts of weddings. Christmas was meant to be special this year, with her sister and Ava there to join them. It had been too many years since they'd all been together for the festive season.

*   *   *

With much cajoling Ava finally settled to sleep. Gingerbread cookies lay on the cooling rack in the kitchen and Dave, Emma and Maddie's father, brought out the port and cheese board.

Emma, glass of port on the rug next to her, sat on the floor putting gifts into stockings. Angela usually did this and it was a tradition that had gone back to when her own children were small. But with the stress of hosting Christmas on top of the fast encroaching wedding, she decided to head upstairs for a relaxing bath instead. The bride to be had taken on the task instead, despite being equally exhausted. It was sheer adrenalin in anticipation of her big day that kept her going.

Christmas hymns on the radio had replaced the comparative jarring of the TV and Maddie shut her eyes, glass of port in hand, and reclined on the sofa. Dave, on the opposite end, mirrored her pose exactly.

Emma stuffed the stockings contently. In went satsumas, candy canes, chocolate coins and nuts. Small presents were wrapped and included. Each member of the family (bar Ava) had contributed a small stocking gift. From previous years of experience Emma could guess some of the little parcels might include socks, toiletries, earrings or cheap gadgets. She had contributed a bar each of her favourite soap; a natural and homemade brand she'd recently discovered and had since used nothing else.

As she compiled the selection of items, she glanced over at the Christmas tree. Smiling, she remembered the incident three years prior, that led to meeting Jed for the first time. It had also been Christmas Eve and after fighting her way into her flat with a wayward tree she'd encountered an angry neighbour. Jed, recovering from a bout of flu and having stumbled across a pile of pine needles strewn across the hall, engaged in a heated exchange with her. Little could she have guessed that less than two weeks later they would be dating.

A lot had changed in those three years since. Less than a year later Jordie, her best friend, had moved out of their shared flat to marry Devon, after a whirlwind romance. Fast forward to Emma and Jed's own engagement and then the sad passing of Jed's mum just two months later, having fought a long battle with illness. The thought that she could not be at her son's wedding had saddened them all. It was also Jed's first Christmas without his mum around and the thought lingered at the back of Emma's mind. They'd decided not to let the sad event cloud their big day, yet thoughts of his mum were inevitable.

O Little Town of Bethlehem rang out on the radio. Looking over at the sofa she saw Maddie sleeping. She contemplated waking her sister, knowing it to be her favourite carol, but decided against it. Maddie finally looked peaceful and relaxed. The tension etched onto her face upon arriving that afternoon had been obvious and Emma hoped she was ok.

Angela had prepped Dave and Emma earlier in the day to not mention the split. It had been a hard few months. No one knew quite how to address the situation, especially as Maddie herself had been so secretive. Emma had no idea what had gone wrong between her sister and husband Greg and she didn't feel comfortable to ask. Their marriage had seemed so solid.

But what, Emma reflected, did she really know about her sister's personal life? It had been a long while since she could honestly say they'd been close. Maddie had moved out of the family home as soon as she was old enough and Emma, being nearly four years younger, had grown used to feeling like an only child during the remainder of her teens.

Maddie had been so keen to spread her wings and fly. She'd left home in her teens and married in her early twenties. Meanwhile the sister's relationship had slid, with only a few occasions where Emma could remember having deep, meaningful conversations, usually involving a couple of bottles of wine. Maddie's relationship with her parents had also changed. There was no animosity between them, yet Maddie didn't share a closeness with them that Emma enjoyed.

Emma had always wanted to stay near the family nest, seeking her parent's advice over important life decisions and visiting regularly, especially when needing a break from city life.

This was to be the first Christmas they'd all spent together in seven years, and the previous time, Maddie had made her exit as soon as it was not considered rude.

Emma had hoped her marriage prep would allow for some bonding time with her sister. But Maddie and Greg's shock split had resulted in less togetherness instead of more. Emma pondered whether Maddie kept her distance for a reason. Perhaps she felt guilty, or ashamed, or even a failure?

So many marriages broke up that Emma knew she had no reason to feel like that, but Maddie was a perfectionist and would likely take the break up as a personal indictment of her character.

Not knowing how to help her sister, Emma returned her thoughts to the suddenly trivial job of the stockings. Aware that the two families were each facing trying times, she hoped the wedding would go some way in strengthening them all.

* * *

Maddie woke to a shrieking daughter, delighted and joyful by the large stocking at the bottom of her bed. Maddie groaned at the early start. The room was still dark with just a hint of grey light illuminating the edges of the curtains. Her own stocking lay heavy on her legs and she smiled. It had been years since she'd last received one.

'Mummy, Christmas is here!' gasped Ava excitedly. 'Look what I got,' she exclaimed, holding up the elongated sock.

'Let me help you open it,' Maddie replied, shaking off her bleary-eyed state.

Together they pulled out the goodies, including a glittery pink hair brush and miniature copy of the Peter Rabbit story for Ava and a bottle of posh bubble bath and purple sequinned woollen gloves for Maddie. They nibbled on their candy canes and chocolate coins as she read Peter Rabbit to Ava.

After the story Ava turned to her and asked, 'When will Daddy be arriving, Mummy?'

'You won't be seeing him today sweetheart,' Maddie ventured, delicately. 'He'll pick you up tomorrow, on Boxing Day. Do you remember Mummy telling you a few days ago? It'll be like having two Christmas days. Won't that be exciting?'

'I guess,' the little girl pondered. 'But I would like Daddy to be with us now.'

'I know honey.'

She held her daughter in her arms as the three year old tucked into her Christmas sweets. Maddie suppressed a sigh. She needed to stay strong. Now wasn't the time to cave into her emotions.

* * *

'Happy Christmas!' exclaimed Emma, scooping up her niece and sliding a pair of antler ears onto her head. Emma wore her own Alice band, with a pair of Father Christmas' on top.

'You look ridiculous,' said Maddie to her sister, coming down the stairs behind them.

'Cheers,' Emma grinned.

Ava touched her antler ears reverently and ran off to the kitchen to show her grandparents. Emma and Maddie followed on behind.

'So, Jed and his family are joining us later?' Maddie asked.

'They're arriving at one for lunch. Just Jed and his dad. His brother will only be arriving on the day of the wedding. He's busy sunning himself in the Caribbean.'

'All right for some.'

'He's a semi-professional footballer. He earns a decent salary'.

Maddie felt Emma was understating it slightly, but didn't say anything. She could hardly judge, having never met Jed's brother. In fact, she had only met Jed himself four times. Considering her sister had been with him three years, it was far from sufficient.

'It'll be nice to meet his dad,' Maddie offered.

They entered the kitchen to be greeted with a cacophony of noise and activity. Big piles of peeled and chopped vegetables lay on chopping boards. The gigantic turkey was prepped and ready to go into the oven. Their father was cranking up the coffee machine which only got brought out on very special occasions. Ava had been put to task decorating the gingerbread cookies from the night before. Angela looked slightly flustered as usual as she buzzed from one chaotic kitchen surface to another. Emma took over the peeling of potatoes, which seemed to have fallen by the wayside. Maddie noticed that all of them were wearing an item of red clothing, a classic Christmas tradition in their family, and she smiled to herself as she picked up a knife to help.

'We'll go through to the living room now and see if Father Christmas has paid a visit,' Angela said, twenty minutes later, when the bulk of the work had been done. Ava squealed with delight and jumped down from her chair at the kitchen table, leaving a sticky icing trail behind her. The others followed, carrying mugs of piping hot coffee.

The living room looked even more festive than the night before, with the addition of a huge pile of presents bunched beneath the tree. The beer bottle and plate of mince pies left out for Santa the night before were both empty. All eyes were on Ava as she ran over to the gifts and bobbed excitedly, a look of expectation in their direction.

'Wait just one minute,' Maddie said firmly, as the rest of the family took seats close to the warm glowing fire. 'Ok Ava, pass me a present.'

It had always been tradition for one to act as 'postman', dishing out a gift to each person before they were opened. Maddie read the tag on the present handed to her and whispered the name in Ava's ear. The little girl laughed in enjoyment and ran to her gran with the package. Moments later they each had a gift in hand and the opening began. Amid the unwrapping, laughter and shrieks from Ava, Maddie heard her phone ring. Seeing Greg's name flash up on the screen, she exited the room and hit the green button.

'Happy Christmas,' came the voice that still managed to give her a little jolt, despite their separation four months ago.

'Happy Christmas Greg,' she replied crisply, annoyed with her betraying emotions. 'Are you wanting to speak to Ava?'

'Yes, in just a minute. I was hoping to speak to you first.'

'Oh?'

'Well, you see... I don't know if you know... Emma sent me a wedding invite a few months back and I said yes at the time, as we were still seeing a counsellor and... well I thought we'd be ok. But now,' he sighed audibly. 'I would still like to attend the wedding'.

Maddie felt a knot in her stomach. She remembered the phone conversation with Emma back in September. Emma had asked if inviting Greg was still ok and Maddie had mumbled a reply somewhere along the lines of 'sure, if you want to'. They had been attending counselling sessions for weeks; something Greg had requested and something that Maddie had tried not to place all her hopes on.

She was too angry, too hurt and too tired of the situation to really expect talking to help. She realised now that she had barely allowed the process to work. She had been determined to hold on to the disappointment instead. That disappointment had turned into weariness and confusion. She kept her feelings close to her chest, not revealing them to Greg, nor anyone else. It was the easiest way to prevent being hurt again and to at least pretend that she was moving on.

But recently with the holidays and the wedding looming, Maddie found it harder to hide those insecurities and Greg's threatened appearance worried her. Yet she also felt guilty, knowing that Emma and Greg had known each other years and it was only fair that she'd want him at her wedding.

'I... I really don't know if that's such a good idea. It would be confusing for Ava to have her dad there and yet not be there with you properly. If you see what I mean?' she ventured, trying to sound confident.

'Well I could sit with you both? At least for Ava's sake?' Greg sounded so hopeful, Maddie had a sudden urge to cry.

'I think we should stick with the original plan. You have Ava tomorrow and then again on New Years' Day. We can arrange our calendars beyond that,' she hated how cold she sounded, even to her own ears.

'Right,' there was a long pause. 'I guess I'll see you tomorrow then.'

'Yes,' she whispered. She called Ava, who chatted happily with her father for a few minutes before running back to her presents.

After a stilted goodbye he had hung up and Maddie stared down at the phone for a long time before heading back to the living room.

* * *

'We're here! With presents!' Jed's voice boomed through the open front door as he and his father stepped inside, both kissing Angela on the cheek as she let them in. An icy chill followed after them and she quickly shut the door.

Emma enthusiastically greeted her fiancé and Maddie smiled tightly. Her sister was acting like a lovestruck teenager. Maddie hoped Emma was prepared for marriage and how hard it could be. But, of course she wouldn't be, Maddie mused, no one was ever really prepared for that. Hadn't she herself been over the top in love and naive for what lay ahead? Wasn't that why it was a shock when things did start to go wrong?

'Jed's here,' Emma stated the obvious as she led him into the room.

Ava stood shyly behind her mother's legs as the greetings were made. Jed saw her and bent down. 'Here,' he said, handing her a red parcel. 'This is your present Ava. From Father Christmas himself.'

Ava looked at it and then back at Jed with a puzzled expression.

'Oh yes. I bumped into Santa on the way here and he told me to give this one to you. An extra present for being so good this year.'

'But...' Ava began as she tried to process this unusual information. A few seconds passed before she decided to discount it and gleefully accepted the gift, ripping the paper off excitedly and revealing a doll, complete with outfit, dummy, feeding bowls and bottle.

'Thank you!' she squealed.

'You do realise you've just broken two important rules,' Emma laughed, her arms folded.

'I have?' Jed faced her.

'First you lied,' she said this bit with a whisper. 'Secondly you've just bought her affection. She'll love you forever now.'

'I can't imagine why that would be a bad thing,' he shrugged. 'Besides, the lie,' he whispered back, 'is no different to the whole Father Christmas thing itself.'

'I know, I was just teasing,' she put an arm around his waist. 'How's your dad doing?' she asked in a low whisper. Jed turned to look at Harry, who was valiantly engaging in conversation with Emma's parents. The tight, polite smile on his face alerted Jed that he was taking strain.

'It was Mum's favourite day of the year,' Jed confided. 'Dad was always bemused as to why, but humoured her. Now she's not here it's a painful memory. He was very quiet leaving the house.'

Emma looked over at Harry and felt a pang of sadness. She'd grown fond of Jed's father. He was a quiet, reserved man, highly intelligent and generous. Jed was like him, although more outgoing in personality, more like his mother had been.

'If it gets too much, I've offered to take him home. I'll chat to your mum and explain, so we don't appear rude,' Jed said. Emma nodded in understanding. 'I'm hoping the wedding is a positive distraction, although we're all going to be upset that Mum won't be there.'

Jed's face fell as he said this and Emma wrapped her arms tightly around him. It was all she could do to comfort him. Words had long ceased to be enough.

'Anyway,' Jed said, pulling himself together and hugging her back. 'In just two days we'll be on the eve of our wedding day. The following morning, I can finally call you my wife.'

Emma smiled up at him, happiness dancing in her eyes. She couldn't wait to start married life with Jed. It was all she had thought about for months. Life had changed a lot since she'd met him. No longer married to her work, and desperately unhappy as a result, she was now enjoying life.

Being with Jed had opened up a side of Emma that had lain dormant in the mundanities of everyday life. A side of her that she'd forgotten about; the thirst for fun and adventure.

Whether it was 4x4ing in Jed's new Land Rover, taking windsurfing lessons, or simply snuggling on a sofa with drinks and their books at a favourite coffee shop, it didn't matter; what was important was she finally experiencing the life she wanted.

'So, Jed, what can I get you to drink?' Angela said, breaking Emma's reverie. 'We have port, red and white wine, a few beers, soft drinks and tea or coffee. What will it be?'

Jed placed his order while Emma sidled over to Harry. He was looking down at Ava who was showing him her brand new doll, a look of amusement and fondness on his face.

'Harry,' Emma greeted him with a side hug. He turned to her and smiled. 'The young love Christmas almost as much as my June did.'

'I know,' Emma's voice came out in a croak.

'But we mustn't worry on that today,' Harry brought himself up sharp. 'There's lots of joy to be had the next few days.'

She knew he was making the effort for her and she felt touched. It must have been so hard, yet he was willing to put aside his own feelings for the sake of his son's happiness. Feeling the tears prickle at her eyes, she sniffed back her own wave of emotion. They stood chatting with Ava for a few minutes before Angela announced that the dinner was about to be served.

In the dining room, Emma glanced over at the spread on the table before them. The classic Christmas additions were all there; gold and red Christmas crackers, fresh holly surrounding the candle centrepiece, a massive trussed up turkey with two types of stuffing, piping hot roast potatoes, gravy and vegetables and the obligatory Christmas tunes playing on the radio in the corner.

She took her seat next to Jed who squeezed her hand encouragingly. Harry sat on Jed's other side and Maddie and Ava placed themselves on the chairs the opposite side of the table. Dave and Angela sat at either end.

As crackers were pulled, food was served and promptly eaten, Emma smiled, thrilled that the family were coming together so well. Flashes of what her big day would be like entered her mind and she happily joined in with her father's toast to Christmas and family.

*   *   *

Maddie forced down the admittedly succulent turkey, her appetite suppressed by her tumultuous feelings. Greg's phone call had rattled her, leaving her feeling both angry by his presumptions and grim by her own far from amenable response. Add to that her sister's happy display of togetherness and borderline sickly-sweet glances at her fiancé, and Maddie had had just about as much as she could take. Christmas was already proving difficult to swallow, with Ava's innocent wonderings as to where Daddy was. Maddie just wanted the day to end, the wedding to be over and done with, and to head home to lick her wounds.

There hadn't been many nights since the split, where she had fallen asleep without tears, or needed sleeping pills to aid her. The nights always seemed harder than the day, when she could busy herself with work, running after Ava's needs and general day to day tasks. But in the evening, it all caught up to her and there was no more running away to be done.

Her mind would invariably try to process what had gone wrong. Where they could have tried harder and made a better go of it. She felt sick to the stomach at the shot of guilt coursing through her, every time she looked into her daughter's eyes after Dad dropped her home again. The look of confusion and sadness that he couldn't stay and 'why, Mummy, doesn't Daddy live here anymore?'.

And now, on Christmas day, a day for family and fun and Maddie felt wretched that Greg and Ava were missing out on each other and Emma was busy preparing for a marriage, seemingly believing it to be built on roses and sweets and fluffy bunnies, and not on the reality of what it was really like.

She hated how cynical her thoughts were becoming, but knew she was seeing life through the opposite end of the spectrum than Emma. She had been there, where Emma was now; full of naive excitement of the future, thinking only of honeymoon filled days, new homes and eventually the pitter patter of little feet. There was little, if any, thought of late nights arguing, resentment silently building and the colossal mistakes which would leave deep cracks beneath the surface.

But maybe Emma and Jed had it right. Maybe Maddie and Greg had messed up, but Emma and Jed would be the lucky ones. But then, Maddie didn't believe in luck. She believed in hard work and trusting instincts and choosing to persevere. So, had she been too quick to call it a day, when Greg's responsibilities increased at work, leaving Maddie and Ava alone more in the evenings and at weekends? When quiet resentments had led to barely a word spoken, unless in anger. When it was clear the marriage was in trouble, and Greg had responded by booking them a counselling session, she had had the opposite response, withdrawing further from him and calling the sessions a waste of time.

Had she given up too easily? She suddenly felt very sick. She looked around at the family, eating merrily, even Harry despite his grief. She felt even worse at this. Here was a man learning to live without the woman he loved, putting on his best face and getting on with it. At that moment, Maddie couldn't bear the confusion of her thoughts any longer, and coughed suddenly, before standing and exiting the room.

Emma and Angela looked up, both concerned by Maddie's quick departure.

*   *   *

She washed her face in cold water, hoping to eradicate the evidence of her tears. She hadn't cried for a long time. Feeling equally embarrassed and bereft, Maddie attempted to pull herself together. She just had to keep going for a few more days, she told herself sternly. That was all. She had held it together for far longer than that before.

'Mads, are you alright?' Emma gently knocked on the bathroom door. Maddie suppressed the urge to bawl again.

'Yes,' she croaked. 'Just powdering my nose,' she cringed at the ridiculous cliché, which she knew Emma would never believe for an instant.

'Right…' Emma paused. 'If you need to talk….'

'Nope,' Maddie managed to sound nonchalant. 'All fine in here, thanks.'

Emma shrugged, returning to the dining room and wondering what on earth was happening to her family. Everyone seemed to be on edge and barely holding it together. She wasn't stupid, realising the reason for that being her wedding. No one wanted to spoil the big day. She sighed. She had enough on her plate, but that didn't stop her worrying nevertheless. She wished she knew how to help Maddie, but the distance between them over the years prevented her from knowing how. She simply didn't understand her sister's personality enough.

Angela exchanged glances with Emma as she returned. She knew her elder daughter well enough to know when to leave alone. The whole family were shocked by Maddie and Greg's split and were still processing the little information they knew. She quietly vowed to take her eldest out for a meal after the wedding, and then to ask her some pointed questions. She couldn't help her without knowing the full story, but now was simply not the time. She realised, with a stab of shame, that she should have done this months ago, when the split first happened, but had become so focused and consumed by Emma's happy news, that she had missed her other daughter's major life event.

Of course, Maddie had tried to handle it all on her own, as usual, being deliberately vague on the details and insisting that she was fine. It was Maddie's way. But that didn't excuse Angela's quick acceptance and subsequent backing off, and she knew it. Angela put down her fork and placed her hands in her lap, suddenly ashamed, as Maddie returned to the table. Her daughter had clearly been crying, but had once again disappeared behind the mask of self-resilience and gave nothing of her turmoil away.

When the main course was finished the Christmas pudding was brought out. Everyone tucked in, the adults adding generous dollops of brandy butter on their portions. Emma noticed Jed and his father talking in hushed tones. Harry looked tired and subdued. He wore a tight smile and his shoulders were hunched. She stopped eating and looked at Jed, concerned.

Jed gave her a small smile and shook his head. Harry was beginning to struggle. As soon as the last spoonful of pudding was consumed, Jed cleared his throat.

'Thank you, Angela and Dave, for the wonderful meal. We've both enjoyed it, but I think I'm going to take my dad home for a rest. It's been a big day.'

'Oh, of course dear,' Angela responded quickly, having been primed by Jed earlier. 'It was wonderful having you with us this year.'

Harry nodded tiredly and they all stood to make their goodbyes. Emma fought down the disappointment creeping in, trying to remember that Harry's happiness was more important than her own in this moment. But she had been looking forward to spending the whole of Christmas day with

Jed and was saddened that it was being cut short.

'Hey, I'll see you at the rehearsal tomorrow evening,' whispered Jed into her ear.

The vicar had agreed to squeeze the rehearsal in on Boxing Day, not usually done, but with the wedding day so close to Christmas, one of the limited options. She immediately felt bad by her reaction to Jed leaving early. Tomorrow they would be rehearsing their wedding day, only to then spend the rest of their lives together. She could let this one day go, surely?

'I can't wait,' she whispered back, resting her head briefly on his shoulder as they hugged goodbye.

* * *

The rest of Christmas day involved a lot of lying on the sofa, pouring drinks, surreptitiously eating titbits of leftovers, despite being completely stuffed full from lunch, and playing games. Ava was put down for a nap, at which the adults took their cue and also dozed sleepily, either on the sofas, or in Maddie's case upstairs next to her daughter.

As evening fell more food was placed on the dining room table. Cold meat, cheeses and crackers were laid out, alongside Christmas cake and nuts, still in their shells and waiting to be cracked open. No one was really hungry, yet none could resist picking at the food. More games were played and the remainder of the chocolate coins consumed.

Much later Maddie took Ava upstairs to get ready for bed. The little girl placed her head in the crook of Maddie's neck and breathed sleepily. She helped her get dressed and brush her teeth, before placing the exhausted three year old under the covers.

'I hope you had a happy Christmas,' Maddie asked, not expecting a reply, Ava's eyes having already shut.

'Yes, Mummy, 'came the sleepy response. 'And I get to see Daddy tomorrow.'

The simple statement, meant with no intent or persuasion, caused Maddie's heart to break. She kissed her little girl goodnight, made her way to her own bed and wept as silently as she could into the pillow.

* * *

The morning light was as grey and tepid as the day before, but still a great relief from the heavy blanket of night. Emma stirred, turning her head to the lightening curtains and remembered with great excitement that her wedding rehearsal was only hours away. There were still a million little things to do in preparation for the big day and only two days left to get them done. But Emma honestly didn't mind. Now Christmas was passed all she had to focus on was the wedding and finally being able to call herself Jed's wife.

She dressed hurriedly, making her way downstairs to the kitchen. Maddie was hunched over her phone, catching up on the news headlines, nursing a cup of coffee. Emma could hear Ava playing in the front room with her new toys.

'Have you two been up long?' Emma asked, pouring herself a coffee from the coffee pot on the side.

'Hmmm, since about six,' Maddie mumbled, still looking at her phone. Emma noticed how tired she looked and realised it probably wasn't just due to the early start.

She sat at the kitchen table, holding her coffee cup between both hands. Her mind was full of jobs she still had to complete: cutting up the printed name places, putting sweets into bags for the favours, putting ribbons around the tealight holders which would make up the centre displays on the tables.

Rather than the expense of outsourcing those jobs, Emma and her mum had spent the last few weekends adding the personal, and finishing, touches themselves. As a junior health care worker, marrying a University lecturer, the budget was tighter than she'd ideally have liked. But admittedly she had enjoyed making the decorations, putting her own style into the wedding, as well as the bonding time she'd had with her mother.

Her thoughts drifted to the wedding dress that was hanging in her wardrobe. She'd collected it the week before and couldn't help regularly peeking at it. It was an ivory gown, made from taffeta, with a beaded bodice and full skirt. Delicate beaded straps completed the dress. It was decadent yet still classic and Emma utterly loved it. It was worth her entire savings, even if she'd only wear it one day.

Maddie's and Ava's bridesmaid dresses had also been collected, alongside Jordie's, Emma's former flatmate and long term friend. She hadn't seen Jordie since the final dress fitting six weeks ago and she looked forward to catching up. Jordie had married Devon a while back, but hadn't seemed to move out of the honeymoon phase, having more or less disappeared off the face of the earth.

Maddie stretched and yawned, before properly focusing on Emma for the first time. She smiled and joined her sister at the table.

'Excited for the rehearsal?' she asked, injecting as much enthusiasm into her voice as possible. She'd made a decision over the sleepless night to make Emma's wedding a priority, which would hopefully prove a wonderful distraction from the mess she'd made of her own marriage.

'Yes,' Emma replied, the element of surprise in her voice.

Have I really been so self-absorbed? Maddie thought ruefully. Even Emma doesn't expect me to be positive.

'I've got all these jittery nerves that don't know if they want to bubble up as excitement or explode in panic,' Emma laughed. 'But I do know that I am so ready to marry Jed. I can't believe it's so close, yet it still feels ages away.'

'Oh, it'll go quick, I promise you,' Maddie offered. 'Especially the wedding day itself. I can barely remember mine now, there was so much going on it was a bit of a blur.' It felt weird talking about her own wedding, yet strangely comforting too. Other than Ava's birth it was the best day of her life. Even if she couldn't remember much of it, she remembered the feelings of joy and excitement. She remembered the thrill at becoming Greg's wife and she knew Emma would be feeling exactly the same about Jed.

Emma played with the now empty coffee cup and sighed lightly. 'I feel like I'm on the cusp of something brand new and huge. In a way it can't come quick enough, but it's nerve wracking too. To be honest, I just want the day to be here now.'

'Soon, very soon,' Maddie smiled, her hand squeezing Emma's. They grinned at each other. It had been a long time since they'd last sat and talked like this. It was nice.

'Mummy,' shrieked Ava, running in from the other room. 'I'm hungry.'

The moment broken, Maddie reverted to her role as mother, while Emma returned to the coffee pot for a refill.

*   *   *

'Daddy's here, Daddy's here!' Ava shouted, as a car rode over the gravel outside.

They were seated in the living room, the effects of Christmas day still weighing heavy on their energy levels. No one had much of an appetite, bar Ava, and had just picked at leftovers in the fridge and generally hung around the house all morning. Maddie had tried not to dwell on the inevitable arrival of her ex and deliberately thought of other things instead. But now it seemed the time had come.

The next couple of minutes seemed to hang in the air uncomfortably. Finally, the doorbell rang. Ava was a flurry of shrieks and giggles as she followed Angela to the door. Maddie stayed back, uncertain.

She heard, rather than saw, Greg embrace his daughter and spin her around. Ava's happy yells brought on a peal of laughter from her father and a minute later they both entered the living room.

Maddie forced herself to meet his eyes, noticing how tired he looked.

He ran a hand through his sandy blonde hair and nodded a greeting. The difference between his response to Ava and Maddie was palpable. He was still upset about the phone call, she guessed, cautious how to greet her and perhaps feeling awkward amongst those he'd long considered family.

Emma cleared her throat and approached him with open arms. 'Greg, Happy Boxing day,' she attempted with gusto. He hugged her in return, before accepting Dave's welcome immediately after. Angela hovered in the doorway behind, watching her older daughter's reaction carefully and thoughtfully.

There was a brief and uncomfortable silence. Greg was the first to break it, turning to Ava and whispering, 'Father Christmas visited my house too, darling. There's some presents waiting just for you.'

Ava jumped on the spot excitedly and Greg scooped her up. 'Sorry to head out again so quickly, but I've planned a few things for Ava, so we must get going,' he paused briefly. 'Could I have a word Maddie, before we leave?'

Maddie, having avoided eye contact without even realising she was doing so, lifted her head in surprise. 'Uh, yes, sure,' she stuttered. Greg passed Ava to Angela and they headed into the hallway for some privacy.

'Look, I know this is going to be awkward,' Greg began immediately, keen to get his piece across. 'But I really think I should be at the wedding. I know what you're going to say…' he interjected quickly, 'but Emma is still family and I really want to see her get married.'

Maddie hugged her arms around herself and sighed. 'It's ok Greg,' she said. 'I actually think you should be there too,' she wasn't about to admit this was because she had felt guilty ever since the phone call.

'You do?' he looked relieved and surprised. 'Well, that's good…' he hovered uncomfortably. 'I also… um… I know I'm not part of the wedding party, but Emma did also mention that I'd be welcome at the rehearsal, which I believe is tonight?'

'No,' Maddie felt a twinge of irritation. 'I don't think that's necessary.'

'But I have to drop Ava off tonight anyway, so I might as well meet you all at the church.'

'Have her for the night then,' Maddie stated impatiently. 'There's no need for you to be at the rehearsal.'

'Regardless, I'd like to be,' Greg replied firmly. She saw the determined look in his eye and felt her anger rising. Why was he being so stubborn? She understood him wanting to come to the wedding, that was fair enough. But he had nothing to do with the rehearsal and was simply using Ava as an excuse. He knew Maddie would have no problem with Ava staying over and returning her the following morning.

'I'll see you there then,' he finished with a determined tone. He turned back to the living room to collect Ava and Maddie stayed back, fuming. She didn't look at him as he left the house, their excited daughter in tow. She headed to the kitchen to try and cool off.

Taking a deep breath, leaning against the countertop, she closed her eyes. She knew there would always be awkward interactions between them, but this simply felt like scoring points for the sake it. Yet Greg wasn't usually a vindictive man. Perhaps the Christmas situation had pushed him too far?

'Are you ok?' Emma had quietly entered the room and placed a hand on her sister's shoulder. 'I heard the conversation. I don't want the wedding to cause any friction between you.'

'Oh Emma, there's already friction, please don't blame yourself for that. Greg's just getting back at me, that's all.'

'Do you really believe that?'

'Why else Emma? There's no other reason,' Maddie sighed, squeezing her sister's hand and leaving the kitchen looking defeated.

Emma watched her go. She had a sneaking suspicion that Greg's behaviour was less an attempt to upset Maddie and more a last desperate reach for reconciliation.

* * *

'I can't believe my best friend is getting married in two days!' Jordie arrived in a blast of volume and enthusiasm, brightly dressed in a myriad of bold colours. The entire ensemble was rather alarming and certainly woke up the sleepier of the family, still induced by the festive food and drink on offer.

Devon followed in behind, his boy band floppy hair and good looks bringing their own dramatic entrance. They were a ridiculously good looking couple, Emma grinned to herself, as she embraced her friends. They had arrived for the rehearsal, which was thankfully, for Emma's waning patience, only a couple of hours away.

'Can I see the dress?' Jordie asked excitedly.

'Oh, I think we should wait until the wedding day for Emma to show it off, don't you dear?' Angela stepped up, aware of Jordie's tendency for the over dramatic and at time, inappropriate requests.

'No… I meant mine,' Jordie gave a slight pout before recovering, as Maddie, behind her, rolled her eyes.

'Um, sure,' Emma conceded.

The women headed upstairs and Angela took the hanging bag of dresses out of the wardrobe and unzipped it carefully on the bed. Emma touched the soft, lightest grey, tulle bridesmaid dresses, a smile playing at her lips. It was almost time.

'Great,' exclaimed Jordie. 'I'm going to need to try mine on. I have to make sure it still fits now that I'm pregnant.'

The reactions to her, almost flippant, statement were instant. Emma gasped, surprised and a little lost for words. Angela flew a hand to her heart, the fluster already appearing on her cheeks as she began to panic that they'd be a bridesmaid short, due to a too tight dress and no time to alter it. Maddie simply looked thunderous. They'd all been so careful to keep this time about Emma and her good news. A bridesmaid announcing a pregnancy was completely ill timed and selfish. At least it hadn't been announced on the wedding day itself, mused Maddie, a small blessing she supposed.

Jordie, completely oblivious to their reactions, fingered the dress nervously. ''I really hope it still fits. My jeans have felt a little tight this week.'

'You're… pregnant?' Emma stuttered, having managed to find her voice again.

'Yes, about eleven weeks. I'm having the first scan in the new year.'

'Wow. You never said anything,' Emma couldn't help feel a little hurt. Despite their opposite personalities, they had at some time been close.

'Sorry, it's just been so busy the last few weeks. We've put the flat on the market. We'll need somewhere bigger now.'

'Right,' Emma paused. 'Well congratulations. That's amazing news. We best try this dress then. Hopefully it'll still fit fine.' She turned to see Maddie's furious expression and chose to ignore it. Jordie wasn't everyone's cup of tea, but she didn't want any falling out so close to the wedding. They'd all just have to get along.

Jordie headed off to the bathroom to change, leaving the other three in an awkward silence. Angela looked ready to combust with panic. Emma dared not meet either woman's gaze, knowing at least one of them would take it as a sign to express their feelings. Several minutes passed before Jordie returned and Angela let out a loud exhale of relief.

'It looks fine,' she exclaimed. The dress still hung beautifully, despite a slight tightening across the middle. Providing Jordie didn't develop a bump in the next two days, it'll be alright.

'I feel like a whale already,' Jordie moaned, at which Maddie harrumphed and left the room. 'What?' Jordie looked around, confused.

'Nothing,' Emma said airily, smoothing out Jordie's dress in an attempt to distract her. 'The dress looks lovely on you. You can't notice a difference.'

'Oh, I hope not. Although I am obviously excited about the baby. I'm just not looking forward to putting on weight.'

Angela gave her a small smile and waved away Jordie's concern. 'Well, that's enough drama for now. I'm glad the dress is fine. I'll leave you two alone for a bit and go put the kettle on.'

Jordie looked herself over in the mirror, oblivious to the tension she'd caused. Emma had flashbacks to their time together as flatmates. Emma had been a lot more serious then, her job demanding hours and energy beyond what was healthy. In a weird way Jordie's flighty personality was a type of tonic, balancing out Emma's more serious moments. Emma was grateful to Jordie for bringing a lighter aspect to her life, even if she still held the potential to rub everyone up the wrong way.

Emma was genuinely pleased for Jordie though. She didn't mind the news of the baby so close to the wedding, although she did wish Jordie had shown a little more tact. Jordie didn't mean it maliciously, but wasn't known for her good timing.

'Anyway,' Jordie waved away her bombshell, 'how are you feeling about the wedding? I remember being so nervous just before.'

'Surprisingly ok at the moment,' Emma admitted. 'I just want the day to hurry up, it seems to be taking forever to get here.'

'Well, this evening will make a difference. The rehearsal is like the last big thing before the main event.'

'It's going to feel so weird practising our vows, knowing we won't really be married yet.'

'Don't worry,' Jordie said, looking intently in the mirror at her makeup. 'It won't feel real. You'll know the difference. Besides you won't be wearing your dress. Only then will you feel like a bride.' Emma had to admit Jordie was right. Nevertheless, the rehearsal would go a long way in making the wedding seem real and with it just around the corner Emma felt a bubble of excitement begin to build.

*   *   *

'Are you ready for this?' Maddie asked, as she and Emma stepped out of the car into the freezing night air. Their breath formed clouds of steam as they hovered, cold hands in pockets, waiting for the others to arrive. To Maddie's right stood the pretty church, illuminated by lights in the grounds, its bell tower proudly dominating the icy sky.

'I think so. I have butterflies,' Emma said nervously.

'You'll be fine,' Maddie replied, squeezing Emma's hand. 'You'll be doing this for real in two days time. This is the easy bit,' she baulked as she realised how that came across. 'Sorry, I meant that in a good way. I'm not too brilliant with the marriage advice right now.'

Emma wanted both to console her and to probe her sister about the separation, but their parent's car, carrying Jordie and Devon as well, suddenly swung into the small car park, followed immediately by Jed's. As everyone disembarked from the vehicles Maddie gave a heavy sigh and Emma followed her gaze to another car approaching, realising it must be Greg and Ava.

Ava ran from the car into her mother's arms and Greg slowly crunched his way across the gravel path. He raised his gaze to Maddie's, aware that she wouldn't be best pleased by his appearance. She refused to give him the satisfaction and nodded civilly. Maddie wasn't about to make a scene at her sister's rehearsal. She'd take the high road. She walked into the church, Ava in her arms whispering about how amazing her day had been with Daddy, and sat down in the front pew.

Emma and Jed approached the front of the church, holding hands nervously and excitedly as the vicar greeted them and began to run through the order of the service. Angela and Dave watched on, smiling at Emma proudly, Jordie and Devon and Jed's best man Felix stood to the right of the happy couple.

The vicar then explained who needed to stand or sit where and at what order and part of the service to do so. Maddie could see Emma desperately trying to remember everything, a slight look of panic across her face. Maddie wanted to reassure her. It always seemed a bit daunting when first hearing it, but the vicar was used to guiding couples through the process.

Next Emma and Jed began their practice vows. Maddie shifted uncomfortably in the pew. She had a sudden flashback to her own wedding and remembered her joy at saying the words she'd longed to say, since the day she'd met Greg. She knew she'd marry him on the very first date. It was weird, not exactly like a thunderbolt, more a steady certainty that this was the man for her.

Despite herself, she looked across at him now. She almost jumped out her skin as her eyes met his. He was watching her intently and a muscle twitched in his jaw. She lowered her gaze instantly, the shock causing her heart to thump wildly in her chest. Embarrassed and more than a little confused by her reaction, she made sure to keep her attention on Emma and Jed, as they completed the mock vows.

As they filed down the aisle Maddie wanted to kick herself. Why was she so emotional all of a sudden? They had separated months ago and she had felt the decision was for the best. Greg had become distant and difficult to live with during those two years after accepting his promotion. He seemed to live for work and Maddie often felt like a single parent. She hadn't thought that actually becoming one would have made much difference.

She wondered if it was purely Christmas, and the first one spent apart, that was causing all the emotional upheaval she was now feeling. But the truth was she had had a heavy burden of guilt, failure and grief on her shoulders ever since that fatal conversation. She could never forget the look of pain on Greg's face as she broke the news that she and Ava wouldn't be coming home and she felt they should officially separate.

Maddie had ignored the fact that neither had yet served divorce papers.

The time of year was a busy one and she'd mentally put it off until the start of the new year. But now she wondered if there might be another reason behind her procrastination and felt instantly confused and stressed out.

She had never wanted her problems to encroach on Emma's big day. She needed to sort herself out and focus. Pondering on what ifs was destructive and unhelpful, not to mention distracting and she took a deep breath to steady her thoughts.

* * *

Emma reached the end of the aisle and stopped to grin at Jed. Having practised their vows, she felt giddy with excitement and felt the nerves melt away. She could do this. In fact, she couldn't wait for the real event.

She glanced at the bridal party behind them and took in their own excited expressions. As her gaze fell on Maddie her heart dropped a little. Maddie looked stressed, her eyes darting all over the church, almost as if mentally clocking the exits. But more than that, Maddie looked scared and uncertain. Emma knew Greg's appearance had shaken her sister, but couldn't imagine why Maddie should have had such a violent reaction.

Maddie had previously kept a stoic response to the split, not showing her emotions and reassuring family that they were keeping things civil for Ava's sake. No one had received more information than that, and Emma, puzzled, couldn't imagine what had so abruptly changed.

Jed noticed Emma's worried expression and quietly whispered in her ear.

'Are you alright? Not having second thoughts,' he said it in jest, but the slight flash of panic in his eyes gave him away.

'No,' Emma half laughed at his concern, yet a second later resumed worrying at her lip.

Jed followed her gaze to Maddie, who was standing a little separate from the family as they helped themselves to an urn of tea that had been laid on. The vicar was chatting animatedly with Angela and Dave, Ava danced around Greg's legs excitedly and the others sipped their beverages. Yet Maddie looked awkward and hovered uncertainly.

'Do you want to go to her?' he asked softly.

'No…' Emma hesitated. 'I think she'll be ok. Oh, I feel terrible saying that, when she clearly isn't. I just don't know what to say to her. She's been so distant. And I just don't get why she's being like this,' her voice grew angry and Jed quickly ushered her outside the church to continue the conversation.

In the church yard the temperature had dropped even more and they hugged their jackets tightly around them. The crescent moon was bright through the trees and an owl hooted in the distance. Jed turned to Emma, his forehead creasing at her recent outburst.

'Are you and Maddie having problems?' he asked.

'No,' Emma began, frustrated and cold. 'Maybe if we did, we might actually get somewhere. You know what I mean?' she said, at Jed's incredulous expression. 'I might actually know how she feels and be able to help. All I can see is that for some stupid reason they decided to split, when it's clear that Greg at least still loves her, and I think she may still love him too. I can't think of any other reason for her reaction. What I don't understand is why they are just giving up.'

Jed stood silent for a moment, briefly looking up at the moon as he thought. He turned his gaze to Emma.

'You do realise,' he began cautiously. 'That marriage is difficult.'

'Of course I do,' Emma spluttered.

'A lot of married couples don't make it….' he paused.

'Probably a higher percentage of unmarried one's don't either,' Emma said.

'That's most likely true,' Jed chuckled. 'The point I'm trying to make is that we don't know the reasons why they felt unable to go on. But they're hardly alone in struggling to make marriage work. My parents, and I'm sure yours too, had rough years amongst the good. It's not going to be all happiness and roses, Emma. It'll be tough and ugly and raw at times.'

'I know,' she whispered, suddenly feeling ashamed.

'I'd hazard a guess that what your sister needs right now is support and a shoulder to cry on, not our judgements as to what happened. Although her timing is perhaps a bit inconvenient,' he finished, trying to lighten the sombre mood.

Emma sighed heavily. Jed was right. She couldn't begin to imagine how hard the last few months had been for Maddie. She didn't understand the reasoning behind the split, but maybe that wasn't for her to understand. She shoved her hands deeper into her pockets and let out a pocket of breath into the chilly air. Then she looked at Jed, her eyes widening.

'You don't… you're not changing your mind are you?' she asked, her words coming out sharply and in a panic. 'It sounds like you think marriage will be impossible.'

'Not at all. Just that it's real and not a fairy tale. There's no reason our marriage won't last the distance. Besides, I want to experience all of that with you, the good and the tough. We'll work through it all together.'

Emma drew closer and snuggled under his arm. 'Ok. Good,' she replied simply.

*   *   *

The next twenty four hours were a blur. Favours were finished, orders of service boxed up ready, shoes polished. Various family members headed over to the church and reception venue to start decorating. Jed drove to the airport to collect his younger brother Philip.

Angela had pre-prepared a massive lasagne, which she bunged into the oven as soon as the family returned from their various jobs. Jed stayed away, wanting to stick to the tradition of not seeing the bride too close to the wedding.

Emma, anxious with anticipation for the morning, could barely manage a bite of her dinner. Maddie, sitting opposite, had the same problem. Her mind was full of unanswered questions about her own marriage.

Angela glanced between her two daughters. With one about to begin her married journey and the other seemingly about to end hers, Angela wondered what advice she could give to each of them. She knew Maddie kept her cards close to her chest. She was unlikely to open up, even to her own mother. What could Angela really say to her, that would have any real impact? Or perhaps it would, but Maddie would never show evidence of it.

Emma, on the other hand, would accept the advice politely, perhaps even enthusiastically, but wouldn't necessarily think it need apply to her. In some ways the two sisters were more alike than they realised.

Angela wished they both realised that marriage took work. That it was normal to run into problems. It was normal to sometimes resent the other and not appreciate them fully. That, just like with a house, or a car, a relationship needed maintaining and looking after. If it was left, it would rust and crack, and what were small issues to fix would become huge and costly. She wasn't sure either daughter understood that completely. But then, neither had she as she'd embarked on the journey. Only decades of marriage had taught her that.

Emma finally gave up pushing food around her plate and gave a sigh. She looked up at her mother and smiled tightly.

'Butterflies,' she tried to explain. 'I feel so nervous all of a sudden.'

'It's perfectly normal. Tomorrow is the culmination of months of planning. It's a new chapter for you and Jed too. There's bound to be anticipation,' Angela said.

'Yes, your mother was terrified to marry me,' Dave chipped in. 'According to her mum and dad, they had to coax her out of a locked bathroom before she'd agree to get in the wedding car. She was forty minutes late to the church.'

'Yes, well,' Angela said shortly, giving Dave a warning glance. 'That was a bit different... for... many reasons. But Emma isn't going to feel that strongly, right my dear?'

Maddie spluttered from the other end of the table. 'What reasons Mum?

Seriously, I'd love to hear this,' she leaned forward, a mischievous smile on her face. 'Were you really thinking of not marrying Dad? I mean, I had nerves on my day, but I was determined to marry Greg….' She trailed off, her sudden playfulness forgotten. Even saying his name was causing an ache in her chest. What was wrong with her?

Not realising the change in tone, Angela grimaced at her own choice of words and the avid audience in front of her.

'If you must know…' she tried to say flippantly, and failed. 'I was young, only twenty two. All my friends were already married. I know it's hard to believe these days, but then it was normal. So, when I met your father, I was excited that it was my turn. Only…' she paused, collecting her thoughts, and thinking how best to explain it.

'I guess I got a little anxious on the day that I was about to commit to a lifetime together. It suddenly seemed very real. I was genuinely in love with your father,' she shot Dave a fond look. 'But a little part of me was terrified to be signing up with something so… final.

'People didn't get divorced as much in those days. It really was a final kind of thing. So, I got a little scared… But I've never regretted a moment since,' she said happily. 'Marrying your father was the best decision and I'm glad I did.'

'Right, pass me your plate Emma, if you've finished,' and with that Angela expertly changed the subject as years of parenthood had taught her to do.

Maddie looked at Emma, then across at Dave, and suppressed the urge to giggle. It was surreal to think of their mother having had doubts. Emma grinned back at her sister, feeling suddenly a whole lot better about her own nerves. Dave carried on eating his dinner, as nonplussed as a man secure in his relationship could be.

*   *   *

The morning of the wedding was sunny and bright. A crisp, fresh breeze had blown the grey winter clouds away. It was still cold, but the bright orange globe in the sky was a welcoming and cheery sight.

Emma had woken after a surprisingly deep sleep, a jolt of excitement coursing through her and spurring her out of bed. She stood in front of the full-length mirror assessing her still bleary appearance. Today she would become Jed's wife and she couldn't quite believe the day had arrived. All the anxiety and build up over the months would now cease to be.

She felt at peace, no longer fretting or nervous. Indeed, even the butterflies had subsided. Now she just wanted to get started. She wanted to wear her dress, walk down the aisle, see Jed again and say the vows that ushered in the rest of their life together.

She heard a soft knock at the door and Maddie stuck her head into the room. 'Oh good, you're up. Mum's prepared some breakfast, although you may not be up to eating, of course. I can however offer some Prosecco or Bucks Fizz if you'd prefer?' Maddie smiled, giving her sister a quick hug.

'Breakfast and a drink sounds nice, actually,' Emma smiled back. 'I think I've found my appetite again.'

'I'm impressed,' Maddie said. 'On my wedding day I couldn't eat all day. I was more excited than nervous, but I still couldn't manage even a bite.'

'Well, I barely ate yesterday, so I'm ravenous now!'

'Good morning, my darling,' Angela slipped through the open door and embraced her youngest daughter. 'I can't believe my little girl is getting married today.'

Emma rolled her eyes. 'Mum, I'm thirty one.'

'You'll always be my little girl, Emma,' Angela hugged Emma's shoulders and approached the dress, hanging from the wardrobe door. 'Oh, you're going to look like a princess.'

'Shall I bring up the tissues?' Maddie laughed. 'Mum's going to be crying all day.'

'Too right I am,' Angela bit back a hiccup. 'I've earned that right.'

'You'll spoil your makeup,' Emma warned. She gave her mum a quick hug. 'Shall we go eat?'

Down in the kitchen Ava was tucking in to an egg and a plate of soldiers. Dave kissed Emma on the cheek as soon as she walked in, squeezing her in one of his breathless hugs.

'My little girl...' he said, gruffly.

'First Mum, now you,' Maddie teased.

'I can't help it. You'll be the same over Ava,' he replied.

'Oh, well, that's the thing. Ava isn't allowed to get older and get married, ever,' Maddie stated. 'So, I don't have to worry about that, do I?'

Dave harrumphed. 'It'll happen whether you like it or not. Do you think I wanted either of you to grow up and move out?'

'I'm sure you had your moments,' Maddie replied, at which Angela nodded behind her. 'Charming Mum,' she laughed.

'Well, I'm just being honest,' Angela shrugged.

Emma sat down next to Ava, taking a glass of the offered Prosecco and a slice of toast.

'Looking forward to being a bridesmaid today?' she asked the little girl.

Ava smiled an eggy grin and nodded enthusiastically. Emma ruffled her hair fondly. 'It's a big day for both of us, isn't it?'

Maddie stood at the counter, a cup of coffee in hand, and grinned. It was nice seeing her sister bond with Ava. All the years Maddie had tried to be independent from the family, trying to prove she could hold it together and make it on her own, she now realised were in error. She'd sacrificed much of her relationship with them. It had been unnecessary and she knew that now.

No wonder she'd struggled to open up with them after her separation. Maddie had pushed them away so long that she hadn't even known how to bridge the gap. But the simple act of her sister getting married had allowed that to happen. Emma and her inclusive, generous nature had aided the process. Maddie hadn't had to beg to be back in the fold, or even apologise for years of staying away. She had simply been accepted by them all, no questions asked.

She realised they had a lot of unanswered questions. She was willing to try and answer them, when the time was right, and felt grateful she hadn't been pushed. She also realised how amazing her family was.

'Right, I must get showered,' Angela announced suddenly, shaking Maddie from her reverie. 'I'll make sure I'm not long Emma, so you can get in there as soon as possible. When is Jordie arriving?'

'Only at ten. She seemed quite concerned that she'll be arriving the same time as the hair and makeup lady,' said Emma. 'I had to reassure her that there would be plenty of time to get ready and no one would get missed out.'

'She's such a drama queen,' Maddie tutted under her breath, at which Angela shook her head and frowned.

'Shhh,' Angela mouthed quietly. Maddie dropped her gaze and drank the rest of her coffee. 'Well, I'll be down in ten minutes Emma.'

'Thanks,' Emma replied through a mouthful of crumbs.

The doorbell rang and Maddie looked up. 'That must be the florist. No one else is due yet.' She left the kitchen, answering the door to the young florist Jeannie, who looked barely old enough to be out of school, let alone old enough to run her own business. Maddie ushered her in and Jeannie carried the long box through to the kitchen.

Emma squeaked in excitement and even Dave couldn't help crowd round for a look. Jeannie lifted the lid. Inside was Emma's bouquet, a mixture of deep red roses and evergreens usually seen on Christmas wreaths and displays. Sprays of conifer and yew leaves, with trailing reddish and green ivy, complimented the roses and occasional sprig of white baby breath.

Two smaller, matching bouquets joined it. They were for Maddie and Jordie. Ava had the privilege of holding the basket of red rose petals, ready for the guests to shower the newlyweds with.

'Do you like them?' asked Jeannie tentatively.

'Oh, yes,' Emma's breath barely a whisper. 'I love them. They're exactly what I'd hoped for.'

'I'm so pleased,' smiled Jeannie. 'I have the corsages in the van for the groomsmen and of course, you Dave. I'll bring them through, then I must dash to the reception venue. I was able to decorate the church last night, but I could only get access to the reception this morning.'

'Thank you so much. You've done such a wonderful job,' Emma grinned, struggling to pull her gaze from the bouquet.

Now she'd seen the flowers she realised it was all happening. With the wedding only a few hours away, her dream of marrying the man of her dreams was about to come true. She was almost stunned by the idea, despite the build up of previous weeks. It just seemed so matter of fact now; it was about to happen and she just had to go along for the ride.

Emma picked up her bouquet and held it to her nose, inhaling the sweet smell of the roses. The bouquet was heavier than she'd thought it would be. It felt solid. It was in complete contrast to the intricate adornments of the wedding; such as the decorations, favours, and even the delicate design of her dress. And yet its solidity made the whole day seem realer still.

The next hour flew by. Emma enjoyed a quick shower and sat in her dressing gown with a cup of tea, as both Jordie and the makeup lady Anna arrived. The photographer Ian also turned up as Anna was applying the eyeshadow, and he snapped away unconsciously, capturing the informal moments between the bride and bridesmaids.

Ava looked lovely in a cream sequinned dress, with full taffeta skirt. A faux fur light pink stole and sparkly white shoes completed the look. Emma and the adult bridesmaids also had stoles, but in white.

Angela joined them, wearing a pale lavender dress with delicate silver embroidered flowers trailing down its length. Maddie gave her mum a big hug.

'You look beautiful Mum,' she whispered.

Angela squeezed her daughter back, giving a contented smile.

'As do you, sweetheart.' It had been a long time since she'd received a compliment from her eldest. Indeed, it had been almost as long since Angela had given one to Maddie. They had never been particularly well received in the past. She didn't understand why, but felt grateful that her daughter seemed to be thawing towards them all.

Thirty minutes later Emma was helped into her wedding dress. As the tiny buttons were done up, Emma smiled at her mum, who had tears in her eyes. Maddie, Ava and Jordie were dressed in their bridesmaid dresses, and the five of them embraced.

They headed downstairs, Emma assisted by Maddie, who held the train of the dress aloft. As they reached the bottom Dave exited the kitchen and took in the sight before him.

'Oh, my Emma,' he choked. Unashamedly wiping away a tear, he drew his youngest daughter into his arms and gave her a tight hug.

'Dad! My bouquet will get squashed.'

'I'm sorry, I'm just so proud of my girl.'

'The car is here,' Maddie interrupted, as she heard the vintage rolls Royce pull up on the gravel drive outside.

And just like that, it was time to go. Emma smiled sheepishly at her father, who squeezed her hand in return.

'Come on, my girl. Let's go get you married,' he said huskily. And out the door they went.

*   *   *

The small and picturesque church was packed full of friends and family. Small sprigs of baby breath and evergreen decorated the ends of the pews. The church itself was pretty and quaint, with classic stain glass windows and pillar candles dotted around inside. It hadn't needed much adornment beyond the flowers.

The groom and groomsman nervously hovered, waiting signs that the bride would be arriving. Jed hadn't slept much the night before, the anticipation building with each hour. He couldn't wait to see Emma. He couldn't wait to marry her either. But he was incredibly nervous, not helped by the gentle ribbing about getting married that he had received from his brother.

He wasn't at all concern by the teasing, nor his decision to marry Emma. He just wanted to get the day going, to say his vows and be able to call her his wife. But all the waiting suddenly made him feel flustered. He knew if Emma could see him, she'd laugh. He was normally the steady one, helping calm her anxieties.

He caught Greg's eye, who was already sat five pews back, looking nervous himself. They both gave small smiles of encouragement. Jed liked Greg. He had only met him a few times, but he seemed a genuine, family kind of man. He wasn't about to get in the middle of Greg and Maddie's issues, but he could see that Greg was at the wedding for more than just supporting his sister-in-law.

The guests were filing in steadily, filling the pews and looking around expectantly. Emma was due in just a few minutes, but as the bride, it was of course her prerogative to be late. He hoped for his nerves she wouldn't be too delayed.

After what seemed an age, but couldn't have been more than ten minutes, the doors at the side of the church opened and Wagner's Bridal Chorus erupted from the organ. Jed turned suddenly to look and from the distance saw a glimpse of his wife to be.

She was radiant. His heart beat wildly as she slowly approached, her father walking her down the aisle. Emma beamed as she saw him and he couldn't help but return her grin.

This was real. This was happening. He couldn't have been more excited.

*   *   *

Maddie reached the front and lined up next to Jordie and Ava. She looked down the length of the church knowing Greg would be there. As her gaze settled on him, she felt a pang of anxiety. He was dressed smartly and had had his hair cut, though his usual stubble still remained.

Seeing him sat there alone tugged at her emotions. It felt out of place somehow. It didn't quite feel right seeing him sat on the side lines, when he should have been amongst the rest of the family.

She sighed quietly, so as not to distract the enraptured bride and groom. The last few months had been so hard. It seemed so cruel and unfair, to Ava mostly, but also to all of them. Divorce had always been something that happened to others, a part of life really. Now that it was possibly happening to her, it seemed ugly, raw and distressing.

Yet, she knew friends who had been relieved to divorce, to be able to leave an unhappy situation and make a new life for themselves. But she and Greg had had some incredible times. Their marriage had had many happy years. So why did it all have to go wrong? Could she really have done something to salvage it?

She felt his gaze on her and she looked up slowly. She knew instinctively that he was thinking of their own wedding day. There was so much promise on that day. Now... she just didn't know anymore.

Thinking about it was exhausting. She hated that she couldn't just detach herself and enjoy her sister's wedding. She had been so controlled over the weeks and now she was struggling to hold it together. Perhaps if Greg had decided not to come to the wedding, she'd have been ok. But Maddie had begun to question her separation before that. Indeed, she'd never felt truly sure of her decision. A heaviness in her gut had followed her around since September.

The wedding, it seemed, was just a catalyst. All the memories she had of her own wedding, coupled with Greg's presence, added to an uneasiness inside. That uneasiness had been growing ever since they split.

Maddie felt the sudden instinct to run and had to physically force herself to stay put. Bubbles of anxiety squirmed inside her stomach and she battled to keep her composure. A brief glance in Greg's direction showed concern on his face. He knew her too well. He could see she was struggling. In a way, that made it worse. He knew her. He knew everything about her. There was no getting away from that. She couldn't hide anything from him.

The vicar motioned for the bridal party to take their seats. Forcing herself from those uncomfortable thoughts, she sat and tried to focus on Emma and Jed's vows. Emma looked radiant. All nerves forgotten, she repeated the vows quietly but confidently, with Jed smiling on as if not believing his luck.

Jordie, looking on, unconsciously rubbed her still non-existent bump. Dave and Angela also sat in the front pew, tears glistening in both of their eyes. Ava fidgeted a little uncertainly next to Maddie, and she reached out an arm to steady her daughter.

Harry, Jed's father, watched his son from the other side. He looked so proud and every so often his right hand would pat the wooden pew, as if aware that Jed's mum should have been seated beside him.

It made Maddie's heart ache for him. Yet, despite the sadness, he was clearly thrilled for his son. Philip, Jed's brother, sat next to Harry and glanced across at his dad from time to time. Maddie was touched by how caring and considerate both sons were towards their father.

For the first time she couldn't understand why she had wanted to be so independent from her family. Their support, their understanding of who she was, the community they created, it all made far more sense than trying to walk life on her own.

The whole family were there, Greg included, to witness Emma's big day. It was a happy event, a bringing together of two families, yet also birthing a new branch of Emma and Jed's own family unit. This was unity. All their foibles, all their issues, all together, loving each other and supporting one another through it all.

Emma finished her vows and couldn't help grinning as Jed recited his. It was finally happening! They would be husband and wife in just moments. Three years she had waited for this day, knowing he was the one she wanted to be with. Now the day was here and she couldn't have been happier.

As Jed completed his declarations, the wedding rings now securely on their fingers, the vicar continued the ceremony. He concluded by announcing them husband and wife. Jed drew Emma into an embrace and they kissed, while friends and family clapped and cheered.

Angela let forth a sob, having held in her emotion the whole service and Dave laughed as he threw an arm around her in merriment. Ava squealed happily, although not understanding what had really happened.

Harry and Philip patted each other on the back and Jordie smiled serenely, quiet for once, as she caught her own husband's eye. They smiled at each other as they thought of their unborn child, due to arrive in only six months.

Maddie risked a look in Greg's direction. He was looking across at Emma and Jed, clapping along with the rest of the crowd. She removed her gaze and dropped her head slightly. She had a lot of soul searching to do, she knew it. But for now, she would just enjoy her sister's moment.

*   *   *

After what felt like a million photographs, the wedding party moved on to the reception, at a beautiful sandstone manor house. The room they had chosen had two large bay windows, with French doors in between, which opened up onto neat and stunning gardens.

With the light already beginning to fade outside, the candles which made up the table decorations added a cosy atmosphere, casting a warm glow around the attractive room.

Guests seated themselves at the circular tables, while the bridal party sat at the long rectangular head table. All the tables had evergreen centre pieces, matching Emma's bouquet and giving the room a festive look.

Maddie sat down at Emma's left and watched Greg, the other side of the room, showing Ava all the pretty decorations. He had been a star during the afternoon, keeping their daughter entertained while Maddie posed for photographs and helping Emma get into position for hers.

Maddie realised she was glad he had come to the wedding. Not simply for his help, but also because he belonged there. He was part of the family, regardless of what they were going through personally. He'd been a son and brother-in-law for many years and she realised that really wasn't going to change.

Greg began to head back across the room, holding Ava's hand and swaying it gently. Ava giggled as she danced along. He caught Maddie's eye and nodded. She nodded back self-consciously.

She turned her attention to Emma, who was busily trying to take her seat, grinning at everyone who stopped to congratulate her. Emma finally plonked down, looking exhausted, and exhale deeply.

'Big day?' Maddie asked with a laugh.

'Oh my, the biggest,' Emma sighed again. 'I'm worn out!'

'You look so happy,' Maddie took a sip of her champagne, ignoring the slight pang at her own unhappiness.

'I am. Oh, that sounds really smug, doesn't it?'

'You're allowed to feel smug on your wedding day.'

'Good. I will then.'

The sisters laughed and both took a sip of their drinks. Emma looked across the room at her new husband, who was regaling some friends with an hilarious anecdote.

Jordie and Devon were nowhere to be seen, Jordie having complained of feeling a bit nauseous shortly after their arrival at the house. Emma hoped she was ok.

Angela and Dave were busy greeting long lost relatives, the type that you only ever bump into at weddings or funerals.

Emma turned to Maddie and observed her for a moment. Her sister looked lost in thought. She had held the same expression for most of the day and Emma wondered what was going on. She understood that Maddie hadn't wanted to bring her personal troubles into Emma's wedding day, but Emma felt the time was right to ask.

'How are you really doing Maddie?' she plucked up the courage to ask.

Maddie looked surprised for a moment, before trying to hide her concerned expression. 'Oh, I'm fine... really, I...' she paused and seemed to sigh inwardly, her shoulders drooping.

'Oh, Emma, I'm not really fine. But,' she added hastily. 'I don't want to discuss this on your wedding day. Today is about you.'

'But when are we going to get a chance otherwise?' Emma asked pointedly. 'I'll be off on my honeymoon and you'll be heading home. We live a two hour drive from each other, we both work full time and you're a busy mum. Even if we make more of an effort to spend time together, we both know it's not going to be discussed in a hurry. So, what better time than now?'

'You don't want to hear about my marital woes when you've just got married. How depressing!' Maddie gave a short, unconvincing laugh.

'Ok, don't tell me the entire story here, if you're not sure. But at least answer my question truthfully,' Emma pressed, aware that if Maddie didn't open up to her now, it may never happen.

Maddie paused, watching Greg as he was caught up in a fairly stilted conversation with some cousin-in-law, twice removed. Ava was busy crouching beside him, inspecting the sequins on her shoes.

'Greg...' Maddie began, taking a deep breath. 'I guess I felt that Greg had replaced me with work. She had become his mistress, if you like, if not his actual wife. It felt like I had been demoted. Ava too at times.'

'I thought I was making the right choice, when I walked away. It had been going on too long, we'd both grown resentful of each other, and I couldn't see a way out. But... I think, maybe I was too fast to give up. Oh,' Maddie groaned. 'I don't know. I just don't know. Greg wanted counselling. I went along, but convinced myself right at the start that it wouldn't work. Maybe if I had given it a chance....' Her voice broke and she couldn't continue.

Emma grabbed her hand. 'Do you still love him?' her voice barely a whisper.

'I told myself feelings didn't matter, that I was choosing with my head this time,' Maddie eventually replied, still casting odd glances toward her estranged husband. 'But the last few weeks, especially the last few days, have made me wonder if I made the right choice...' she paused again, thinking.

'Yes... I do still love him. Quite a lot actually,' she laughed harshly and instantly bowed her head in anguish. 'Emma,' she said, her voice broken. 'I think I've wrecked our chance to save our marriage.'

'You need to talk to him, Maddie,' Emma urged. 'You might think that, but what if he's still willing to make it work.'

'Oh, Emma,' Maddie sighed. 'It's never that simple. Even if we did get back together, he's still in that job. Things would still go back to the way they were. Then we'd be in the same boat. No, I have to believe we split for a reason.'

Emma shook her head at this. 'Maddie, if you talk it through, maybe you can compromise. Make choices that will prevent this happening again. How do you know unless you sit down and try and work it out?'

Maddie considered making a remark about Emma having just got married and naivete and then thought against it. Firstly, it would be cruel on her wedding day to criticise her knowledge of marriage. Secondly, Emma was actually right. Despite the simple advice, it was good advice nevertheless. The only problem, Maddie mused, was whether she and Greg had left communication and compromise too late.

'I'm sorry I brought all this up on your happy day,' Maddie smiled sadly, squeezing her sister's hand. 'I have a lot to think about and shouldn't be dragging you into it.'

'I'm your family,' Emma said. 'Greg's too in fact. I want you to come to me and talk like this, even if it is on my wedding day!'

Maddie smiled and took another deep swig of her drink. Looking across at Greg, she made a decision. She would talk to him. Maybe not this evening, but she acknowledged that they needed to talk it through properly, if he was willing.

The evening gradually unfolded, with banter, speeches and raucous laughter around the room. The three course meal was delicious and the toasts were performed with much enthusiasm, especially after the bar was opened.

Ava lay in Maddie's arms, starting to look sleepy, her dessert unusually left untouched. Maddie watched Emma and Jed grin at each other, listened to the speeches and shed a tear, particularly at the short and moving eulogy to Jed's mum.

Outside it was pitch black, except for the fairy lights stringed up through the bay trees and over the pagoda toward the ornamental pond. Inside, the candles released a festive light, beautiful and calming, as the live band began to play gentle jazz numbers.

Emma and Jed stood to take their first dance and Maddie watched them, herself beginning to feel sleepy. She was aware of Greg's eyes on her and she wondered briefly if there may yet be hope, before pulling her thoughts back to the wedding.

Much later, with Ava now sleeping across two chairs pulled together, with her father's suit jacket draped over her, Maddie returned to her own seat and watched the couples dance slowly together.

'May I join you?' she heard Greg's voice close by. She looked up, seeing him stand behind her and she nodded.

'I wanted to thank you,' he said seriously, glancing briefly over to Emma and Jed, still dancing, their eyes only for each other. 'Thank you for not protesting against me being here today.'

'Well, I did a little,' Maddie laughed nervously.

'You could have made it a whole lot worse,' he stated. 'You could have refused point blank and given me hell today.'

'You should be here,' she said simply. She didn't want to say more in case her voice broke and gave away her emotions.

He watched her for a long while, as she pretended her face wasn't burning up under his scrutiny, focusing instead on the dancing and pretty lights. Eventually he cleared his throat.

'I'm sorry I messed up,' he croaked. It was obviously a hard thing for him to say and Maddie was surprised.

'I continued seeing the counsellor, after our sessions had ended,' he spoke quickly, trying to say all he had wanted to for weeks. 'I realised during the sessions just how much I'd hurt you. How I'd allowed my job to be more important than my family...'

'We're all guilty of that at times,' she said, not quite sure why she was trying to reassure him. Perhaps because of her own guilt and failings in their marriage.

'Please don't excuse me,' he said, his voice nearly a whisper. 'I know I hurt you and left you feeling abandoned... I'd like to try and make that right.'

He said this with such force that she knew he'd been wanting to say it for a while. She felt the prickle of tears behind her eyes and she struggled to stay composed. Could... could there be a chance? She almost dared not hope.

'Thank you, Greg,' she replied, before shaking her head at this wholly inadequate reply. She tried again. 'I... pushed you away. You were so busy that I distanced myself from you as much as I could,' she admitted.

'I resented you and I resented the job. I didn't allow you the chance to make it right. I just decided to move on and I shut you out.'

79

As she said this, she let out a stifled sob. Greg squeezed her hand in comfort and she reluctantly turned her gaze to his. She didn't want to look at him, knowing how guilty she felt inside. He'd tried to make it right and she hadn't let him. It was clear now and she just wanted to burst into tears.

'Please don't punish yourself,' he said hoarsely, reading her thoughts. 'I did something wrong and you reacted by doing something wrong. Blame is a two way street. We can both make this right together. If you are willing to give it a try,' he offered, his expression hopeful despite trying to remain guarded.

'Are you willing?' he asked, dropping his gaze as if frightened of her answer.

Maddie looked at him intently. All fears of whether they could make it work were still there, but something had changed. She knew if they didn't at least try she'd regret it forever. He deserved, as a loving husband for so long, the chance to make it right. She hadn't allowed him that three months before, but now he was giving her a chance to right her mistake.

She felt a swell of love for him all of a sudden. It had always been there, underneath the surface, biding its time. She knew now how she felt and she smiled.

As the musicians started to play a popular Christmas song, the soft jazz mellowing it into a romantic melody, she returned her hand to Greg's. She could feel his body tense in surprise as he turned to look back up at her.

'Yes,' she whispered. 'I am willing.'

*   *   *

Emma and Jed swayed together, staring at one another, as the guests danced by, unnoticed by the happy couple. The day had been perfect.

Emma felt a warm glow in the knowledge that not only was Jed now her husband, but their families could now come together and move forward as one. It had been the perfect family Christmas and what better way to celebrate than with their wedding.

They smiled at each other and Emma threw her head back and laughed happily. They continued to dance, amongst the candlelight, as the ones they loved danced alongside.

Outside, with the temperature dropping drastically, a solitary snowflake twirled delicately to the freezing cold patio. Another soon followed, tracing its own unique trail to the floor below.

Before long hundreds and then thousands of snowflakes danced merrily, as if to the music inside, through the cold night air and settled on the white blanket below. The gardens quickly transformed into a winter wonderland, the trees looking like they were caked in frosted icing.

It was enchanting and magical, and the perfect end to a Christmas wedding.

Printed in Great
Britain
by Amazon